The Last Resort

A Speculative Fiction Review Book Published by
SpeculativeFictionReview.com

www.speculativeFictionReview.com

ISBN: 0-9785232-2-9

Cover art by Peter Dingus.

The Last Resort

www.speculativefictionreview.com

Dedication

The Last Resort is dedicated to the millions of baby boomers now contemplating retirement, and where they intend to live out their golden years.

Chapter One

A gentle sea breeze ruffled the fringes of the beach umbrellas where the two men sat on the sportsman's deck of their exclusive golf club. They looked out across the eighteenth fairway to a line of sand dunes, and beyond the dunes, the ocean glistened in the morning haze.

"The twenty million is a serious offer, you say?" Dermot Bollinger asked.

"That's just for openers, Dermot. God knows what their final offer will be."

Mort Fiddlemore no longer referred to himself as a real estate agent. His business card described his profession as *Realty Analyst and Property Investment Adviser.*

"But it must be a vacant possession," Fiddlemore added. He paused momentarily to admire the gold bracelet on his wrist. "You'll need to remove the residents and their homes from the site."

Dermot Bollinger twirled the ice cubes in his glass of Cheval Regis with his finger. This was his third for the day and he was beginning to feel light-headed.

"What makes them think they can get the resort rezoned for high-density residential development? Believe me, I tried. There's no way the authorities will rezone that land."

"That's not our problem, Dermot. Our objective is to find a way to get these old bastards and their crappy prefab houses off the estate."

Bollinger glared angrily at Fiddlemore. "My homes aren't crappy, they're well built. Christ, I pay my builders a fortune to produce the bloody things."

"Ah yes, but you must still be making a sizeable profit from each home you sell."

"That's because I sell the resort, Mort, not the house," Bollinger replied.

"But you also charge them seven grand a year to live in your resort." Fiddlemore shook his head. "Dermot, you're sitting on a gold mine."

"True, but then I have to play nursemaid to a resort full of whining geriatrics, and that's a pain in the arse."

"Well, you'll need to resolve the problem if the sale's to proceed. Why don't you just tell the old bastards to take their homes and find some other residential park to live in?"

"The resorts are the marketing tool I use to sell my houses. I've got three other projects in various stages of development, and I don't want any bad publicity."

"So the question is, can your tenants and their houses be moved from Serenity Quays without a public outcry?"

Bollinger was thoughtful for a moment—an idea had begun to fester in his mind. "There is something that may work."

Fiddlemore studied his old friend closely. They had orchestrated a number of major land deals, and each had made a sizeable fortune from their association together. Fiddlemore delighted in watching his business associate mastermind some plan or project. Completely logical in his thinking, and without care or consideration for anyone or anything, Bollinger's sole objective was to achieve the best bottom-line result. Profit was his sole motivation, and his drive to make money almost equalled Fiddlemore's own financial ambitions—almost.

Bollinger's gaze had settled on a nearby fairway, and when he finally spoke, it was more to himself than Fiddlemore.

"I could move them all to our residential park on the Tweed Coast."

Fiddlemore leant forward in his chair, fascinated by his friend's comment. "How would you do that?" he asked.

"It's a long shot, Mort, but leave it with me for a day or two and I'll let you know what I'm planning." Bollinger rose unsteadily to his feet. "Now, how about that game of golf? If I have another whisky, I won't be able to see my ball."

* * *

Felicity Grimes smiled broadly at her visitor as she meticulously arranged the few items on her highly polished desk. Felicity tended to be somewhat compulsive about her work habits, an obsession that irritated most people.

Today, as always, Felicity maintained her composure despite her annoyance at being forced to open the site office forty-five minutes earlier than usual.

Felicity was the Resident Manager of Serenity Quays, a residential park on the far north coast of New South Wales. She lived in a company house near the entrance to the complex—a short distance from an imposing set of steel security gates that protected the resort from the outside world. Attached to the front of her house was an office, and in the office window, below a large aerial photograph of the local beach, was a sign greeting visitors to the resort. *Welcome to Serenity Quays, a waterfront paradise for active retirees.*

Office hours were shown on the door, but these were generally ignored because a buzzer had been provided enabling both residents and visitors to summon Felicity at any time, day or night.

Felicity disliked the man sitting opposite her—he was a troublemaker and did not respond to her broad smile or exaggerated friendly manner. She felt nervous when he was around. She sensed he knew exactly how she really felt about him and the other one hundred and thirty residents under her control. Boring old pensioners mostly, who constantly complained about the resort and the way it was run. How pathetic, Felicity though. At her age, living in a demountable home in a retirement village.

Felicity's visitor was Jack Creighton, or Major, as his friends called him. Creighton had been an officer in the Australian regular army, and the title had stuck after he was discharged in the seventies. He and his wife were retired, and long-term residents of Serenity Quays. Felicity could see that the Major was angry—and she knew why.

The Major was an avid golfer and played several times a week at the local country club. He bought his home in Serenity Quays because the property required little maintenance, which gave him plenty of time to play his beloved sport. Serenity Quays also had its own driving range. Originally, the driving range was nothing more than rough bushland, but the Major, with help from several of his friends, had turned the scabrous piece of land into an outstanding par three golf hole. They created the fairway, a putting green, built sand bunkers, and even planted trees on the site. The reason for the Major's anger was the rumour that the owner planned to close their golf facility and build homes on the site.

"The rumours are still persisting, Ms. Grimes, that you intend to demolish our mini golf course."

"I don't attend the Tenants' Committee meetings, Major, but I did hear some residents are concerned there is a danger from flying golf balls," she replied.

"The subject has never been raised at any of the meetings I've attended, Ms. Grimes."

"As I said, Major, you'll have to speak to the Tenants' Committee about the matter."

"The Tenants' Committee is run by a bunch of lackeys. They only do what you and Bollinger tell them to do."

Felicity Grimes looked at her visitor over the top of her glasses. "Major, comments like that could get you into serious trouble, so, for your sake, I'll ignore what you just said."

"I suggest, Ms. Grimes, that you know what is planned." The Major leant back in his chair. "Do you deny your boss is trying to close our one-hole golf course so he can build homes on the site?"

Felicity's face reddened. "I told you, Major, the golf area is creating a serious danger for our tenants, and their safety is paramount."

The Major laughed. "You don't give a stuff about the safety of your tenants, Ms. Grimes, and no one I have spoken to has any concerns about wayward golf balls. In fact, all the nearby tenants love the golf range, and they will oppose your plans to build homes on the site."

Felicity remained silent for a moment as she struggled to regain her composure, then she picked up the phone. "Please leave, Major. I don't wish to discuss this or any other matters with you any further." She began dialling a number. "And Major," she said, pointing at him, "I'm advising my employer you forced your way into my office out of business hours and were abusive towards me." She managed a conciliatory smile. "And another thing, Major. I'll be seeking a restraining order banning you from this office."

The Major rose to leave. "Don't bother, Ms. Grimes. Talking to you and your mates on the Tenants' Committee is a waste of time anyway. In the future, I'll take my complaints straight to Consumer Affairs."

Chapter Two

The small group of people sat around a table on Tony Bloom's verandah at the rear of his house. Like all the homes in Serenity Quays, his deck overlooked one of the man-made canals that flowed through the resort.

Tony and Evy Bloom had been residents at Serenity Quays for five years. They spent much of their time caravanning around Australia, and Serenity Quays suited their lifestyle because their home was secure and their garden was maintained during their absence. But things had changed in recent times, and the Blooms were alarmed by a series of cost-cutting decisions made by the management of Serenity Quays.

Together with some of their friends, they formed a small action group made up of people outside the resort's Tenants' Committee. Those involved shared the same opinion about the devious owner of Serenity Quays, and the failure of the Tenants' Committee to properly represent the residents.

"So, is it true what we are hearing about our golf course?" Tony Bloom asked.

"Management wants it closed on the grounds it's a danger to the residents," the Major replied.

"That's absolute rubbish." Gerry Curry spoke firmly. "Bollinger wants the land so he can build six new homes on the site."

"Do you have proof of that, Gerry?" Tony asked.

Gerry Curry was a consultant to the construction industry and was aware of most development proposals submitted to the local authorities. "I've seen the building application," he replied.

Jessie Creighton, the Major's wife, banged her coffee mug on the table. "The rotten bastard. There must be something we can do—you three have worked your butts off creating our little golf course."

Tony shrugged. "We're outnumbered, Jessie. There aren't enough golfers in the resort to stand up to Bollinger and his mates on this one."

"What we need is for you to get on that Tenants' Committee, Tony," Sue Curry said.

Tony leant back in the chair and placed his hands behind his head. "It may not be that easy, Sue. Some residents are afraid of how Bollinger would react if one of our group were elected to the Tenants' Committee."

"Why should they care what Bollinger thinks?" Sue asked. "It's the residents who elect the committee."

Tony shook his head. "The majority of people in Serenity Quays don't want any trouble, Sue, and Bollinger's mob has undermined our group so maliciously that we're now seen as troublemakers."

Jessie laughed. "So they're happy to be pushed around by Bollinger and his bunch of lackeys." She sighed. "What's wrong with these people? Don't they realise we're paying too much rent for the services we receive?"

"Most of the tenants just want to live their lives peacefully, without any aggravation," Tony replied.

"And that's what Bollinger plays on," Gerry said.

"Well, I think that many of the residents are fed up with the fools running the Tenants' Committee, and there may be a chance to have Tony elected this year." The Major took a sip of his coffee. "But what we must do is keep his nomination a secret until the AGM."

"Why would you do that?" Sue asked.

"Last year we showed our hand too early, and they ran a hate campaign against Gerry. We also failed to respond to their lies, and it cost us votes." The Major grinned. "This year we'll be ready for the bastards and beat them at their own game."

Evy was intrigued. "What do you plan to do?"

"We need to find some dirt on Quinsy Naylor and his mates on the committee," Gerry replied.

Sue laughed. "Sounds like war."

"When you're dealing with a creep like Bollinger, it *is* war my dear," Tony said.

* * *

Quinsy Naylor felt giddy. He was so stunned by the call that he slumped into his lounge chair. He'd never had a personal phone call from the resort's owner before.

"I have an important matter I'd like to discuss with you, Quinsy. Would you and Muriel like to spend next weekend at our place on Bribie Island?"

Quinsy was overwhelmed by Dermot Bollinger's sudden invitation. He and Muriel had arranged to visit Muriel's mother the following weekend, but this was the owner of Serenity Quays inviting them to his magnificent holiday home. Quinsy was in awe of the resort owner. Bollinger was fabulously rich, with several homes on the Sunshine Coast, a deep sea fishing cruiser, and one of his cars was a Ferrari. Since Quinsy was elected chairman of the Tenants' Committee, he'd had several meetings with Bollinger, but to be invited to his home for the weekend was an honour.

Muriel's mother was in a nursing home, and they had been promising to visit her for weeks. Several previously planned visits were cancelled at the last minute, causing distress and disappointment for the old woman. Now Quinsy was faced with a difficult decision. How would his mother-in-law react when they failed to show up again?

Quinsy hesitated for a moment as he contemplated the dilemma he now faced. "Thank you, Mr. Bollinger, we've nothing important planned for next weekend—we'd love to come."

* * *

Bollinger sat for a moment after he had hung up the phone— he was beginning to implement his plan. Prior to the acquisition of his five retirement resorts, his business investments included a number of childcare centres. Bollinger had discovered that young mothers could be aggressive and were quick to turn on him whenever he attempted to reduce his operating costs. Bollinger smiled to himself. The elderly were much easier to manipulate than young parents and their obnoxious offspring.

Bollinger rose from his chair and moved to a large mahogany bookcase behind his desk. He ran his hand along a row of heavily bound legal books on the top shelf and selected one of the volumes. He grasped the spine and pulled it towards him, causing the front of the bookcase to swing open and reveal a liquor cabinet and a large ornate mirror. Bollinger studied himself in the mirror and gasped loudly. The right-hand corner of his toupee had lifted several centimetres and exposed a patch of pink scalp. He quickly applied some wig glue he carried in his pocket and carefully patted down the toupee. As Bollinger examined his wayward hairpiece in the mirror, a disturbing thought crossed his mind. *Had anyone in the office noticed?*

Dermot Bollinger had once considered a hair transplant, but the procedure could not give him the hair density he wanted. Why, he wondered, had fate been so cruel as to leave him bald from an early age?

Bollinger looked at himself in the mirror for a moment longer, then closed the bookcase and returned to his desk. He flicked through his Rolodex and dialled another number at Serenity Quays.

"Bullpit!" an abrupt voice answered.

"Good morning, Arty, this is Dermot. I'm going to need your assistance again, my friend."

Arty Bullpit's manner changed immediately. "Certainly, Mr. Bollinger. I'd be pleased to help, if I can."

Bollinger hesitated. "Did you say, *'if you can,'* Arty?" His voice had a sinister undertone.

Bullpit gasped loudly. "No, no, Mr. Bollinger, what I meant to say was, I would be pleased to do anything you ask."

Bollinger's voice returned to a more pleasant tone. "Our friend Naylor and his wife are coming up to Bribie for the weekend, and I need you to soften him up a little."

Arty Bullpit felt cheated. He had never been invited to spend a weekend with the Bollingers, and now he was going to be called on to carry out more of Bollinger's dirty work. Not that Arty minded. After all, this was an area where he had a great deal of experience.

"What would you like me to do, Mr. Bollinger?" he asked.

* * *

Five minutes after the Bollinger phone call, Quinsy Naylor was knocking on the door of his good friend and next-door neighbour, Arty Bullpit. He would have been there earlier had Muriel not stopped to fix her make up.

Like himself, Arty Bullpit was a ten quid immigrant who had come out to Australia in the sixties. Both men had little time for the local inhabitants, and had never really adjusted to the Aussie lifestyle. Quinsy's main reason for leaving the UK was to get away from his meddling mother-in-law. Ten years later, and

despite an exerted effort on Quinsy's part to dissuade her, she
joined them in Australia.

Quinsy had formed a close friendship with Arty during the
time he had lived in the resort. Both were former union delegates,
they played bowls together, and each shared an interest in making
their own 'home brew.' Their wives were also good friends and
spent a great deal of time in each other's homes. Both couples
were quite proud of their reputation within the resort for being
people who loved to party, which they did with great enthusiasm
most evenings.

The two couples were also the nucleus of a select and
carefully screened group of friends they had created over the eight
years they had been in the resort. Other residents referred to the
group as *'Bollinger's mob.'* The mob virtually ran the place, and
controlled most of the decision-making thanks to Quinsy's
position on the Tenants' Committee. Consequently, the lives and
needs of this select group were well catered to, particularly now
that they had established a close relationship with the owner.

Quinsy always floated his ideas past Arty Bullpit. Not
because he thought Arty was any smarter than he was. In fact, he
considered the man to be mentally inept. But now and again Arty
came up with some sound suggestions, and he always gave Quinsy
his full support. *A good man to have on your side in a tough
situation*, Quinsy would say to Muriel when they were alone.

What Quinsy didn't know was Arthur Bullpit was a former
employee and standover man for Dermot Bollinger, who used him
to collect outstanding debts and rough up competitors and others
who got in Bollinger's way. Now Bullpit was retired. He had
purchased a house on very good financial terms from Bollinger,
and was living in Serenity Quays rent-free. In return, Bollinger
was able to draw upon his services to control and manipulate
Quinsy and the Tenants' Committee at Serenity Quays.

Arty's wife Buffy answered the door and welcomed Quinsy and Muriel in her usual loud, high-pitched voice. "Darlings, how lovely to see you, come in." Buffy greeted them with exaggerated delight, as if they had not seen each other for years, even though the four had spent the morning shopping together.

Quinsy noticed that Arty was on the phone when they arrived. Arty quickly terminated the call as his wife opened their security screen door.

"We've been invited to spend the weekend with the Bollingers," Muriel Naylor blurted out before she was inside.

Quinsy watched for a look of envy on his friend's face, but there was none. Instead, he seemed quite excited for them. Quinsy was disappointed—he enjoyed his friends being envious of his achievements.

Chapter Three

Alby Titmus sat on the pontoon at the rear of his home and looked out over the still waters of the canal that bordered his lot. Alby loved the position of his house. Unlike the other residents of Serenity Quays, whose houses sat crammed alongside one another, his block jutted out onto a corner of the resort where a large holding lake joined the first canal. This was the main canal that fed the other smaller waterways that meandered through the resort.

Alby had no neighbours at the rear of his property, so he could sit, unobserved, and talk to his animal friends that came to visit him during the day. Alby was lonely, so he enjoyed the company of his companions, though he had difficulty remembering their names. Remembering names had become an increasing problem for Alby—at times he noticed he had trouble remembering his own.

Today Alby was concerned. There had been talk that he should move to a special home where he would receive proper care. Two women had come to his house that morning, or maybe it was the previous morning, and talked about selling his house. One of the women, who insisted she was his daughter, said he was too ill to remain at Serenity Quays. The other woman, the fat one, agreed, and said she would take care of everything—whatever that meant.

But Alby had no intention of leaving Serenity Quays, so he had sought the help of his friend in the Secret Service. The agent always came when he needed him, and this time, he had promised to eliminate the fat woman before she had a chance to do whatever it was she was planning to do. In the meantime, Alby would stay out of sight and concentrate on taking care of the animals that visited him each day.

The largest of these was Boris, who came by every day at sunset. Alby always remembered Boris's name, because he was his favourite. But Alby only ever saw Boris's large green eyes, peering at him from the surface of the lake as he waited for his special treat.

Alby spent much of his day fishing from his small pontoon, and he always had several large mullet for Boris when he called. At dusk, Alby moved to the bank and dangled his feet in the cool water, splashing the surface to let Boris know his meal was ready. Right on time, Boris appeared, his huge green eyes observing the old man as Alby selected the first fish from a plastic bucket by his side. Alby passed the fish to his friend and saw it vanish in a wild rush of water. He waited a few moments, then selected another, passing it just below the surface to his hungry companion.

Alby chatted amiably to his friend about the day's events, and how annoyed he was about the suggestion that he should move to a special home. Alby listened to his friend and nodded in agreement as Boris expressed concern about his evening meal of mullet if Alby were to leave Serenity Quays.

Suddenly there was a loud noise behind them, and Boris slipped from sight beneath the water.

"Go away, Jack Russell," Alby shouted angrily. "I don't want you around here—you frighten my friends."

The small, excitable white and tan dog ignored Alby and rushed to the water's edge, barking loudly at the spot where Boris had been.

Alby rose to his feet, picked up his plastic bucket, and swung it angrily at the dog that was now growling and yapping frantically at the unseen menace in the water.

"You hit my dog with that bucket and I'll deck ya, you senile old bastard," Willy Hogan shouted. Hogan lived in a house nearby, and his dog had become a nuisance around the resort.

"Your dog scares my friends," Alby shouted.

"You don't have any friends, Titmus. You're a crazy old man and they should put you away." Hogan picked up his dog, kicked the bucket containing the remaining fish into the canal, and stormed off down the side of Alby's house.

As Alby watched them go, two wild and sinister looking eyes appeared above the surface. They, too, watched Hogan and his dog depart before slipping below the water.

* * *

Lily Hartmann stared at Felicity Grimes, trying to comprehend what the woman had just said to her. "Are you saying I cannot keep my Sammy?" There was a look of disbelief on Lily's face. "When I come into this place, you tell me I can keep my pet bird until he die."

Felicity Grimes flicked an imaginary speck of dust from her desk. She was becoming frustrated with the visitor to her office. "But you said the bird was a parrot, Lily. Sammy's not really a parrot—he's a sulphur crested cockatoo."

"Hey," Lily replied, rising to her feet. "Where I come from, birds like Sammy, they call them parrots." She dismissed Felicity's comment with a wave of her hand. "You call him a cuckoo if you want, I call him a parrot."

"But Sammy's too big and noisy, Lily," Felicity said. "Other residents are complaining."

Lily Hartmann was almost six feet tall and built like a man. She leant over Felicity's desk and poked her in the chest. "You tell me who complains, and I go talk with them, uh?"

Felicity eased back in her chair, a little overwhelmed by the large woman towering over her. "I cannot disclose the complainants, Lily, but there are a number," she said.

"Probably them little queers down the road or da schmuck next door—what's his name—Fisk? He no like me—always making trouble."

"Because Sammy screeches and swears all day, Lily. And when you let him out of his cage, he terrorises Mrs. Fisk and poos all over her washing. Did you know he gave her a nasty bite on the ear yesterday?"

"That's because she scream when Sammy sit on her shoulder. She scare him."

"Well, the Tenants' Committee wants him removed from the resort, Lily, so there's not a lot I can do." Felicity turned her attention to the neat pile of paperwork on her desk.

"Well, you and your bloody Tenants' Committee will have to take Lily Hartmann to court, then," she replied. "When we buy this house, you say we can keep pet bird until it dies."

"That rule applies to a tenant who has a budgie or a canary, Lily," Felicity said, waving her hands in frustration, "but not for a cockatoo—they can live for a hundred years."

"Sammy belong to my dead husband. I make promise to look after him, even if he lives for one hundred years." With that, she stormed out of Felicity's office and slammed the door behind her.

* * *

Stanley Bancroft was a shy and gentle man who disliked aggressive people and any form of violent behaviour. For that reason, he rarely mixed with the other residents in Serenity Quays, concentrating instead on his main interests—his flower garden and his poetry.

Fortunately for Stanley, his neighbours were quiet, non-intrusive folk like himself. On one side lived Benny and Maurice, two gentlemen friends who were obviously gay, but kind and caring. His other neighbour was Roberto DeAngelo, an elderly

Italian who had recently lost his wife of fifty-two years. While Stanley understood the grief his neighbour was suffering, he envied the lifetime of companionship the old man had shared with a loving partner.

Stanley had not been that fortunate. He had been too shy and lacking in self-confidence to pursue the woman of *his* dreams. Most women terrified him, particularly women like Felicity Grimes, who reminded him of his domineering and abusive mother. Throughout Stanley's adult life, whenever a relationship with a woman began to develop, unpleasant memories had caused him to retreat in fear. Now Stanley was sixty-two years old, and he knew he would never find that perfect woman.

Despite his bouts of loneliness, Stanley was not unhappy with his peaceful lifestyle, and he sensed a feeling of inner tranquillity as he dozed in the afternoon sunshine on his patio overlooking the waterway. As he relaxed, his eyes became heavy, which made it difficult for him to focus on the strange object he now saw floating on the water's surface directly in front of him. The object rolled over and Stanley gasped in disbelief. It was his neighbour, Roberto DeAngelo.

For a moment, Stanley was unable to move. He was hopeless in a crisis, and this seemed like one of those moments. Then Stanley realised there was no one else around to help the old man. He rushed to the water's edge, where he removed his suede slip-ons and his tailor made slacks, and waded out into the canal. He grasped DeAngelo by his shirt collar and dragged him up onto the small strip of sand near his pontoon. When Stanley looked at the bearded man's pallid face, he appeared to be quite dead.

Stanley removed the lump of concrete that was tied to the old man's leg and instinctively began resuscitation. He had little idea of what he was doing. Press down three times, or maybe five, blow into the mouth once or twice, he wasn't sure. He forced open the old man's mouth, placed his own mouth over his, and blew

17

firmly. Then Stanley recoiled in disgust. Mr. DeAngelo had obviously enjoyed a final meal heavily laced with garlic. Stanley took a deep breath and blew into the old man's mouth again, then continued with the chest massage. At one stage, he looked up to see Benny and Maurice watching him, spellbound. As Stanley bent down to continue resuscitation once more, Mr. DeAngelo's body convulsed violently and the old man vomited food and water all over him.

"Call an ambulance!" Stanley shouted to the audience that was growing by the minute. "Already have," someone in the crowd responded. Stanley sat cradling the semi-conscious Roberto DeAngelo in his arms until the ambulance arrived, during which time the old man muttered incoherently in Italian. It was not until the patient was safely loaded into the ambulance that Stanley realised that he was barefooted and in his boxer shorts. As Stanley gathered his pants and shoes and hurried into his house, the small crowd broke into applause.

* * *

"Viagra for two dollars a tablet? You must be kidding, Moose." Marty Fisk scratched his crotch. It was an involuntary action that always occurred when Marty discussed the subject of his waning sexual prowess. "The chemist charged me thirty bucks for six tablets, and there was a doctor's bill on top of that to get the prescription."

"I kid you not, Marty. This is the real thing, and more potent than Viagra—from an American pharmaceutical company. Look at the label."

"How do I know they'll work?" Marty was suddenly interested.

"Here." Moose rummaged through a plastic bag of tablets. "I'll give you a free sample. I guarantee you'll get a hard-on in fifteen minutes, and the tabs are effective for thirty-six hours." Moose hesitated. "There's even a money back guarantee—that's assuming your artillery's in working order."

"There's nothin' wrong with my boys, Moose." Marty adjusted himself again. "When I go to the beach and see some of those young chicks in their bikinis it's…" He was lost in his thoughts for a moment. "Well, you know how it is, Moose. Jo Jo and I've been married almost forty years, and lately, well, she's started to sag in all the wrong places."

"You don't have to explain to me, Marty. Us blokes need all the help we can get."

Both men were silent for a moment, each lost in their thoughts of days long past.

"Where do you get them from, Moose?" Marty asked, as he turned the sample tablet over in his hand.

Moose hesitated once again. "I'm the regional distributor for this mob."

Marty was fascinated. "Is that legal, Moose? These things can kill you if you've got a bad heart."

"That's bullshit, Marty," Moose replied. "I've been taking them for over twelve months, and I've had no ill effects."

"You must be kidding, Moose. With that permanent bulge in your pants, the women in the resort are always talking about you."

Moose was fascinated. "So what're they saying—that I'm a sexy old stud?"

"No, Moose, most of them just say that you're a dirty old man," Marty replied, and chuckled.

Moose glared at his friend. "Well, for your information, Marty, I'm getting my fair share of offers from one or two—let's say—*ladies* who have a need in the resort."

"Yeah, like who?"

Moose grinned. "You'd be surprised, Marty…you'd be surprised."

Moose Dart was annoyed by Marty's remark. Moose considered himself a woman's man, and assumed that his nickname was a tribute to his virility and masculinity. The name had, in fact, originated when a resident highlighted a similarity between Dart's unusual gait and a wild moose he had seen while holidaying in Finland.

A knock on the door distracted them. "Come in," Moose called out to his visitor.

Trinity Du Pont stood nervously in the doorway, unwilling to cross over Moose Dart's threshold. "You have something for me?" she said, eyeing Marty Fisk with caution.

"Sure, Trinity," said Moose, rummaging through a carton that sat on the kitchen bench-top. "My latest stock arrived this morning."

Moose gave a box of tablets to Trinity who, in turn, handed over a twenty-dollar note.

Trinity studied the box suspiciously. "These are definitely the same as the last batch you sold me?"

"Identical," Moose replied, holding up the invoice from his supplier. "Were they satisfactory?"

"They were brilliant," Trinity replied, and hastily departed the scene.

"Trinity is dosing her bloke with Viagra?" Marty asked when they resumed their conversation. "The old bugger must be seventy five if he's a day."

"Just another satisfied customer," Moose replied, with an air of confidence.

The phone rang before Marty could continue. Moose listened for a moment. "Okay, Willy," he said. "A twelve pack for you and a sample pack for Stan Huddle. I'll drop 'em round later."

"Willy Hogan is using the tablets too?" Marty asked when Moose had finished his call.

"Been using them for weeks," Moose replied.

Marty Fisk studied the sample in his hand for a moment. "Forget the sample," he said, getting to his feet. "Give me a box of twelve."

* * *

Stanley Bancroft had showered longer than usual that evening as he struggled to wash away the afternoon's unpleasant experience. There had been a number of congratulatory phone calls from residents, including a lengthy call from Felicity Grimes, who had made her own inquiries into the incident. She told Stanley that Head Office had been advised that poor Mr. DeAngelo must have had one of his turns while standing on his pontoon. "Thank God you were near-by, Stanley," Felicity said. It appeared to Stanley that Felicity was anxious to see the matter closed.

Stanley had eaten his evening meal and washed the dishes by 9 p.m. The day's events had left him exhausted, and he planned an early night. He took the phone off the hook and was about to retire for the night when there was a loud knock on the door.

"Who's there?" Stanley called.

"Open up." It was a loud, aggressive voice that seemed to echo through the house.

Stanley opened the door slightly and looked out at the three figures standing on his front verandah. One was a huge man with a flattened nose and a scar from above his right eye to the bottom of his cheek. He wore the ugliest pinstriped suit Stanley had ever seen. Another man was tall and slender and dressed in a light coloured double-breasted suit. This man had pale, almost white skin, white hair, and pink, sinister-looking eyes that clashed with the large bunch of flowers he was holding. The third man stood in the doorway looking immaculate in an Italian suit that was complemented by a black shirt and yellow tie.

21

"Are you Bancroft?" the man bellowed.

"Yes," Stanley replied, almost in a whisper.

Stanley gasped as the man opened the security door—it must have been left unlocked.

"I'm Ricky DeAngelo," he said, stepping through the doorway. "You saved my Poppa from drowning today." He grabbed Stanley by the shoulders and kissed him on both cheeks. "So now, Bancroft, you and me—we're brothers, right?"

Ricky snatched the flowers from the albino and shoved them in Stanley's hands. "These are for your old lady, okay, and this is a little something for you." He snapped his fingers at the big man, who pulled an envelope from his pocket and handed it to Stanley.

Stanley took the envelope and ushered the men into his lounge room. He was too stunned to speak.

"Bancroft, my Poppa was a very important man in his younger days," Ricky said, as he pulled a leather pouch from inside his coat pocket and removed a cigar. Stanley was about to protest, but thought better of it. Ricky lit the cigar and blew a smoke ring towards the ceiling. "They called him the Godfather when he ran the…the organisation," Ricky continued, flicking some of the cigar ash on the carpet. "Now he wants to live in this shit hole," he muttered, looking around. "But hey, he's my Poppa, so I gotta respect what he wanner do, right?"

Ricky's eyes began to water. "But then Mama up and dies and Poppa—now he wanner die too." There was a sob from the large man with the flat nose and the nasty scar.

"Anyway, you save Poppa's life, so everything is okay, and when he come home from hospital, you gonna keep an eye on him for me, okay?"

He gave Stanley another bear hug and headed for the door.

Stanley watched from his front verandah as the three men got into the limousine parked in his driveway. As the albino started the engine, Ricky leant out the window.

"You want any knee caps broken, just let me know, Bancroft. You and me are brothers, right?" Ricky laughed raucously and waved as the car sped off.

Stanley waved back with the brown envelope still clutched in his hand. He slowly tore open one end and saw that inside was a large wad of twenty-dollar notes.

Chapter Four

"My dog is missing," Willy Hogan said abruptly, as he stood in the doorway of Felicity's office.

Felicity sighed. She had just arrived at work and was not in the mood for Horny Hogan, as some of the residents called him. Hogan had recently made a pass at her and, while she was flattered, she knew that Willy had begun to flirt with all the women in the resort. Willy Hogan, it seemed, was going through some sort of late life hormonal surge, a condition that appeared to have afflicted a number of men in the resort recently.

"Your dog is always getting out, Willy, and other residents are complaining. It craps on peoples' lawns and digs up their gardens. You could be forced to give up your dog if you don't keep it under control."

"I don't give a shit about the other residents; I just want to find my Jack Russell," he said, and raised his clenched fist. "And another thing—if I discover that demented old bastard Titmus has done anything to him, I'll...I'll drown the prick."

"Alby! Why would Alby Titmus do anything to your dog? He loves animals." Felicity was curious; Alby rarely came in contact with the other tenants.

"He tried to belt Jack over the head with a bucket of fish yesterday."

Felicity giggled. The thought of the old man lashing out at the annoying little dog amused her. "Well, I'm sure Alby wouldn't do anything to your dog, Willy. And another thing I'm sure of—if your dog is running loose in the resort, I'm going to receive a lot of angry calls from residents, so I suggest you find him, and quickly."

* * *

Sissy Witherspoon raised her arms in despair. "We need more interesting activities," she said, her frustration clearly evident in the tone of her voice. Sissy was chairing the monthly meeting of the Activities Committee, and there seemed little enthusiasm for any of the suggestions she'd put forward. "We had to cancel our last bridge day, our view club has been disbanded, and only Maurice and Benny are attending the needlework classes."

"What about raising money for a worthy charity?" Agnes Hoskiss suggested. Agnes was a shy individual who tended to speak in a quiet, sometimes nervous manner, which many claimed was a consequence of her thirty-year marriage to Charlie Hoskiss.

"We're pensioners—how can we make a worthwhile contribution to a charity?" Hilary Ottoman mumbled.

"We could raise money by producing a calendar," Trinity Du Pont called from the back of the room.

The chairperson raised her eyes and glared at Trinity over her glasses. Trinity rarely contributed anything at their meetings, and usually chattered annoyingly to those around her throughout the proceedings.

"What sort of calendar?" the chairperson asked.

Trinity examined her long elegantly-painted fingernails. "Like the one in the movie," she replied.

"Last year I got a calendar from my sister in England. It had a different breed of dog for each month of the year," Maude Potter mumbled.

Suddenly there was a loud gasp from the back of the room. "Not that movie we saw last month where those women posed for nude photographs?" Dolly Mott said in a hushed voice.

"The year before she sent me a calendar of birds from the English countryside," Maude said to no one in particular. "Delightful little tits and finches."

"Why not?" Trinity replied. She rose to her feet and smoothed down her clothing—her hands proudly outlining the contour of her rather well formed figure. "I'm proud of my body and I'll volunteer, here and now, to be Miss January."

Maude continued to ramble. "One year she sent me one of old wooden boats—but I didn't like that one very much."

"For Christ's sake, Maude, will you please shut up," the chairperson shouted. Sissy regained her composure and turned to Dolly Mott. "How much did they earn from this, fund raising venture?"

Dolly Mott was now beginning to show some enthusiasm for the suggestion. "Over one hundred thousand pounds," she said.

"That's more than two hundred thousand dollars," the chairperson said, turning to the secretary, Clarissa Van Hooganband. Clarissa was so stunned by the nude calendar suggestion that she had abandoned the minutes.

"Does that mean I have to pose nude too?" Agnes Hoskiss asked nervously as she blew her nose on a lace hanky. "It was just a suggestion—the money for charity thing." Agnes wiped tears from her cheeks. "What would Charlie say?" She trembled slightly when she thought of her husband's reaction to the suggestion.

"Get hold of yourself, Agnes, no one's asking you to do anything." The chairperson assumed her authoritative role and glared angrily at Trinity. "Your idea is a little over the top, Trinity, and I'm shocked that you'd suggest such a thing to the ladies of this community."

"I have a nasty hysterectomy scar on my tummy," Molly Quinn commented from the back of the room. Molly was seventy-three, five feet tall, and walked with a stoop. "If I pose nude, I want that brushed out of the photograph."

A hush fell over the room as everyone turned and stared in disbelief at the tiny woman who had just spoken. Molly grinned and shrugged her rounded shoulders. "Well, a woman has her reputation to consider," she said, and returned to her knitting.

"My Berty and I often walk around the house naked. I'm sure he'd love me to pose nude for a calendar." Now all heads turned towards Maggie Pugh, a large woman in her mid sixties. "The other day he took a photograph of me in the shower with his digital camera," she said, rummaging through her handbag. "I have a colour print here somewhere," she continued, delving into the bottom of her bag.

Now the meeting became silent once again as they contemplated Maggie and her equally robust husband frolicking naked around their house together. There were some audible sighs of relief when Maggie gave up the search for her cherished photograph.

"If there's no further discussion on the matter, I'll put forward the motion that the ladies' committee begin planning a naughty calendar to raise money for a suitable charity. What charity do you want to nominate to be the beneficiary of our calendar, Agnes?"

All eyes turned to Agnes Hoskiss, who now sat nervously chewing on her lace hanky. "I was going to suggest we raise funds for the nursing home on Argyle Street. My mother's there, and they're always struggling for money, but I don't know if this would be suitable..."

The chairperson interrupted Agnes' rambling reservations. "The motion nominates the Sisters of Mercy Nursing Home on Argyle Street to be the recipient of all monies raised from the calendar. All those in favour of the motion?"

Only Agnes Hoskiss failed to vote on the motion as the chairperson looked around the room. "Motion carried unanimously," Sissy Witherspoon called loudly, and the meeting broke up to loud applause.

* * *

Charles Badminton-Smyth sat glaring across the desk at Felicity Grimes. He had been arguing a point of legislation for some time. "But Felicity, the regulations clearly state that a resident's comfort and wellbeing must be respected by other tenants. My comfort and wellbeing are being severely interfered with by this woman."

Felicity gave her usual friendly smile, adjusted her in-tray slightly, and then raised her hand in an attempt to interrupt her visitor's argument. Cantankerous old bastard, she thought. Every day he was in her office arguing about some government regulation regarding the tenancy agreement. He's definitely a *Category 4*, she decided. Why had she encouraged the man to buy into the resort? He plays Brahms and Beethoven all day and speaks with a phoney upper class English accent.

Born and educated in Sydney's eastern suburbs, Charles Badminton-Smyth was the victim of three bad marriages and three former wives, who relieved him almost entirely of his inherited wealth. Forever a 'silvertail,' Badminton-Smyth seemed out of place in Serenity Quays.

Felicity shuddered slightly at the thought of Badminton-Smyth's reaction when he discovered Dermot Bollinger's instructions about lease renewals. Bollinger had faxed her earlier in the day. No leases would be renewed until further notice, and she was to defer any house inspections for the time being. Plans to build six homes on the one-hole golf course had also been shelved. But the most disturbing part of Bollinger's fax was his instructions about the offer from Mr. and Mrs. Hawke to buy lot twenty-seven. 'Commence negotiations with them,' his fax had said, 'but don't sign anything.'

Anyone over fifty-five years of age could buy into Serenity Quays, providing there were no kids, no more than one small animal, and certainly no undesirables. In Felicity's opinion, Morgan and Minty Hawke definitely failed the latter requirement, and their offer had been ignored. Now she had been instructed to call them and discuss their offer. If all sales had been put on hold, why did Bollinger want her to continue negotiations for number twenty-seven—with the Hawkes of all people? Something big was happening, and Felicity wanted to make some inquiries with her contacts at Head Office, but she was stuck with the silly old goat sitting across from her.

"Charles, I fully understand how you feel. I'm not a country and western fan either, but Alison Arbuckle is entitled to play whatever music she chooses."

"But not so loudly, and singing along, out of key, in that high-pitched voice of hers—it's just not acceptable, Felicity."

"To be frank with you, Charles, Alison feels the same way about the music *you* play."

Badminton-Smyth seemed stunned for a moment as he stared at Felicity in disbelief. "Everyone I know loves Beethoven—what's wrong with the woman?"

Felicity sighed and spread her arms in exasperation. "Charles, you and Alison are mature adults, go and talk with the lady."

"How could I possibly have a sensible discussion with a woman whose only interest is country and western music?"

"I'm sorry Charles, there's nothing more that I can do. You'll have to sort the problem out between yourselves."

Badminton-Smyth was about to respond to the dismissive reply when a loud roar filled the air and they both turned towards the sound. The noise came from a Harley Davidson motorbike that was being parked outside the office window. There was a look of disgust on the face of Badminton-Smyth as he watched Morgan and Minty Hawke remove their helmets and swagger up the steps of the office. Without knocking, they entered the room and threw their motorcycle gear on the chair alongside Badminton-Smyth.

Morgan was a large individual with a bulging midriff. His mullet cut hairstyle hung like matted grey twine to his shoulders.

He wore a dark, sleeveless T-shirt and his arms were heavily tattooed. Minty, by contrast, was a small woman with black hair streaked with tangerine, and she wore tight leather pants that silhouetted short bony legs and a sagging arse. They had almost as much metal studded into their faces as they had on their motorcycle jackets.

Simply being in the same room as these people disgusted and appalled Badminton-Smyth. Who were they? he thought. And what business did they have at Serenity Quays? Surely, even some of the more base tenants in the resort would not mix with these people.

"Decided to come straight over when we got your call," Morgan Hawke said loudly, ignoring Badminton-Smyth and the meeting that was already taking place. "So, the old girl in twenty-seven has decided to accept my offer, eh?"

"I'm sorry, Charles, we'll have to continue our conversation later," Felicity said, getting to her feet. She needed to remove Badminton-Smyth from the office as quickly as possible, but he remained firmly ensconced in his chair.

"You aren't seriously considering selling a home in Serenity Quays to these people are you, Felicity?"

Morgan Hawke grunted angrily and moved towards Badminton-Smyth. "And exactly what do ya mean by that remark, you pompous prick?"

"Please, gentlemen," Felicity pleaded, as she stepped in front of Hawke. "Not in my office, if you don't mind."

Badminton-Smyth took the opportunity to struggle to his feet and move out of harm's way to the office door. "I'll be speaking about this incident to Mr. Bollinger, Felicity," he stammered, as he hurried from the office.

"You do that, cobber," Morgan Hawke shouted after him. "And keep your fuckin' opinions to yourself, or me and some of my bikie mates might pay you a visit!"

30

Chapter Five

Father Brendan O'Brien stared at the couple seated in front of him, amused and surprised by the story that was unfolding. Charlie and Agnes Hoskiss had been parishioners of his since they moved into Serenity Quays five years earlier. Charlie was a church prefect and Agnes a member of the church auxiliary. Agnes also spent many hours every Saturday preparing the flower arrangements for Sunday Mass. He had watched Agnes Hoskiss as she went about her chores around the church, and he had secretly admired her. She was a comely woman in her mid fifties, and remarkably well proportioned for her age. Lately, Brendan O'Brien had become troubled when in her presence. He had developed an unhealthy lust for the woman that he was finding difficult to put from his mind. Her simple, child-like innocence fascinated him, and he hated the way her husband tormented and humiliated her in public.

Brendan O'Brien considered himself a liberal thinker and an advocate for the changes in the modern day attitudes of the Church. Consequently, little surprised him. Now, however, he was astounded by what he had just read. This suggestion was so unlike Agnes Hoskiss.

"What made you come up with such an idea, Agnes?" O'Brien asked, holding up a copy of the minutes of the women's activities meeting.

"It all happened so quickly," Agnes replied in her soft, pensive voice, as she wiped the tears from her cheek with a hanky.

"And do you intend to appear in this...this calendar?" O'Brien asked. He flushed with an uncontrollable rush of excitement as he glimpsed a brief vision of Agnes draped naked, as Miss December, across the front pew of his church.

"Of course she won't be appearing in any calendar, Father," Charlie Hoskiss said in an arrogant tone. "Furthermore, I intend to have the motion rescinded and an apology issued to us in writing. This is a reflection on the good name of Hoskiss."

"That might be a little difficult, Charlie, seeing as the minutes show that Agnes moved the motion at a formal meeting." O'Brien leant forward in his chair. "Did you move this motion, Agnes?"

"I guess so, Father. As I said, it all happened so quickly." Agnes drew in a deep breath. "I just wanted to raise some money for the nursing home."

"You stupid woman," Charlie said, turning on his wife. "Don't you realise how you've disgraced us—and the Church— with this outrageous proposal?"

Agnes grimaced with embarrassment and buried her face in her hands. Her husband's anger and all the questioning had become too much for her, and she began to sob.

"Now, Charlie," the priest said, glaring at Hoskiss. "That's uncalled for. Agnes' suggestion was well intended, and God knows the nursing home is in financial trouble."

Brendan O'Brien got up from his chair and walked to the window behind his desk. "You realise, Agnes, that the Church cannot openly endorse this calendar." The priest placed his hand under his chin and became thoughtful for a moment. "On the other hand, if the photographs are discreet, I see nothing wrong with the idea. I watched a video recently where some women in England posed for a similar calendar and raised over one hundred thousand pounds for a local charity…"

"You can't be serious, Father?" Charlie interrupted, jumping to his feet.

O'Brien disregarded Charlie's comment and picked up the phone. "Of course the real problem will be Sister Benedictine at the nursing home. She may not want anything to do with the idea."

"This is outrageous, Father O'Brien. How can you condone this affair?" Charlie turned to his wife. "Come Agnes, we're leaving!"

Agnes ignored her husband as O'Brien spoke into the phone. "Good morning, Sister, this is Brendan O'Brien. I have Agnes Hoskiss and her husband with me, and we've been discussing a fund raising proposal..." O'Brien listened for a moment.

"So you've already heard about the suggestion?" he said, looking at Agnes.

The priest scratched notes on his desk pad as he listened. "Yes...no...of course not." More silence. "Yes, I agree." Then he handed the phone to Agnes. "Sister Benedictine would like to speak with you, Agnes."

Agnes Hoskiss withdrew in horror. The memory of her school days and the nuns who taught her came rushing back. But she was trapped. The priest held the phone towards her while her husband—a self-righteous smile on his face—pushed her forward towards the priest's outstretched hand.

With a trembling hand, she took the phone from Father O'Brien. "Hello, Sister," she said in a voice that was almost inaudible.

Agnes listened for some time, nodding continually, but saying nothing. Finally she managed a few words. "Yes, Sister...no, Sister...I will, Sister...goodbye, Sister."

Agnes hung up the phone and stared at the handset for several moments before her husband spoke. "Well, I hope the good Sister was more critical of you and your disgusting proposal..."

Agnes suddenly gripped both of Father O'Brien's hands tightly. "Sister Benedictine loves the idea and thanked me for suggesting it. She thinks it's a great way to raise money for the nursing home. She also thinks it's a wonderful opportunity for mature aged women to show the world that they're proud of their bodies."

Agnes and the priest stood, hands clasped, gazing into each other's eyes.

"May we go now, Agnes?" Charlie said loudly for the third time, watching with anger and confusion as his wife and the priest appeared transfixed on each other, seemingly indifferent to his presence.

* * *

Felicity Grimes stood in the doorway of her office and watched the Hawkes on their motorcycle as they sped from the resort. She remained in the doorway for several minutes and listened to the speeding bike, its engine pervading the surrounding bushland like the howl of some prehistoric beast as it headed in the direction of the town centre.

Felicity shook her head, as if to clear from her mind the terrible prospect of Morgan and Minty Hawke becoming residents of Serenity Quays. The thought was incomprehensible. What was happening to the place she had worked so hard to create? Felicity was primarily responsible for the tenants who had taken up residence in Serenity Quays. She had carefully organised each sale to ensure the right tenants were selected. Older homeowners, people who could be manipulated and controlled—these were the sort of tenants Dermot wanted. Minimise the number of troublemakers, and force them out where possible, he would say to her. But now something was going on that she wasn't aware of. The acceptance of the Hawkes as potential buyers and all the other sudden changes to Dermot's plans almost seemed as if he were intending to destroy the place. But this was her resort, and Dermot Bollinger owed her an explanation. She picked up the phone and began dialling Bollinger's private number. As she did, there was a gentle rapping on her office door.

"Can we speak with you, Felicity?" someone said in a meek voice from outside her office door.

Bollinger's number was engaged, so she hung up the phone and called to her visitor. "Come in, Maurice."

Maurice and Benny from number twenty-five entered the office and sat huddled together in front of her. Felicity saw immediately that Benny had been crying, and Maurice was holding his hand. "We just spoke with Charles, Felicity," Maurice said in a faltering voice. "He told us a terrible story about those people who just left on that simply awful motorbike."

Screw you, Charles Badminton-Smyth, Felicity thought. Charles had obviously gone straight to Benny and Maurice with his news that the Hawkes were interested in buying the house next door to them.

"What story is that, Maurice?" she asked.

"That you're selling Elsie Parker's house to those horrible bikie people," Maurice said. With that, Benny burst into tears.

"Nothing's been finalised with those people, Maurice, so you can stop worrying."

"But Charles…"

"Charles was wrong, Maurice," Felicity interrupted. "I'm obligated to show anyone through the houses we advertise in the resort, providing they meet the criteria. The Hawkes are over fifty, and they have no pets or young children. If I refused to show them a property they're interested in, I could be sued for discrimination." She reached across and patted Benny's hand. "I decide who buys into Serenity Quays, Benny, and I promise you, the Hawkes will never be your neighbours."

Benny wiped his eyes with a damp hanky, then clasped Felicity's hand. "Thank you, Felicity," he said, and whimpered, "You really are a sweetie."

"See, I told you it was a nasty rumour, cheeky bum," Maurice said, patting his partner on the hand. Benny struggled to smile, but was overcome with a loud, involuntary sob.

Felicity Grimes watched Benny and Maurice from her office door. They both turned and waved to her as they wandered off, arm in arm, towards the security gates. When they were out of sight, she turned to a large map on her wall. Tiny red flags indicated a number of homes that were for sale in the resort. "I'll fix you, Badminton-Smyth," she said viciously, and picked up the phone.

The mobile phone number rang several times before it was answered. "Hello Mr. Hawke, this is Felicity Grimes of Serenity Quays calling. I'm sorry to tell you this, but Mrs. Parker is reconsidering her decision to sell her house and lease." She cringed at the abusive exclamation from Morgan Hawke, then continued. "However, there's another property in the resort that may be more suitable for you and your wife. It's a little cheaper, and it has a tandem garage, part of which you could convert into a workshop."

Felicity smiled at the favourable response. "There's one minor problem, though. You'd be living directly behind the man you had a confrontation with in my office today."

Felicity listened, then chucked loudly. "Yes, Mr. Hawke, I'm sure you could handle yourself in the unlikely event of any problems in that area. So, when would you be able to inspect the property?"

* * *

Gerry Curry stopped at the gates and rummaged in the console of his car for his security card. He hesitated for a moment before swiping the card across the security panel. Today, more than ever, Gerry was apprehensive as he passed through the gates

into the secured area of Serenity Quays. As the gates slammed
shut behind him, Gerry turned down one of the narrow roadways.
On each side of the road, demountable buildings stood like
sentinels, most identical except for the odd variation in design.
They were forlorn looking structures, all of similar dull colours,
with cheap cladding and corrugated iron roofs. The buildings were
jammed tightly together, impeding cool breezes in the hot humid
summers, and blocking out the sunshine during the brief, but cold
winters. When he had parked the car in his garage and turned off
the engine, he sat for a moment, recalling the conversation he'd
had with a council engineer earlier in the day.

Because of his work, Gerry had formed friendly relationships
with various local government employees, and information, much
of it confidential, was often made available for his perusal. Now
something very disturbing had come to his attention. Gerry had
been shown evidence of a Queensland property developer's
application to have the land in Serenity Quays rezoned. He was
advised that the company was negotiating to buy the resort, which
they planned to change from a residential park with low cost
housing, to an up-market, canal type residential development. The
proposal, if it were to proceed, would require the removal of all
tenants and their homes from Serenity Quays. Until he was sure of
his facts, Gerry decided that he should keep this information to
himself.

Chapter Six

The day had turned out to be a fabulous experience, far beyond the expectations of Quinsy and his wife. They had spent most of Saturday on Bollinger's cruiser, sipping champagne as they travelled around the waterways of Bribie Island. Now they were seated at the dining table enjoying a meal of Lobster Mornay, prepared by Bollinger's cook. She had interrupted her weekend break, they were told, because the Bollinger's were entertaining special guests.

Quinsy was experiencing a deep feeling of euphoria, a reaction to the attention he was receiving and the expensive wine he had consumed during the magnificent meal. Muriel was intoxicated and had become completely incoherent.

Bollinger had been waiting for the right moment. All evening he had been heaping praise on Naylor for the job he was doing as chairman of the Tenants' Committee.

"Quinsy," Bollinger said, holding up his glass and studying the texture of the fine cognac they were drinking after their meal. "I believe you and I have established a close personal relationship since you were elected to the committee."

Quinsy was imitating his host, but saw nothing special about the wine in the oversized glass he was holding to the light. While he expressed an exaggerated appreciation of the aperitif to his host, he actually detested the stuff, and was longing for a cold glass of his own home brew. He lowered his glass, and was about to reply, when Bollinger held up his hand to interrupt him.

"I'm going to tell you something, Quinsy, that's caused me a great deal of anxiety lately."

Even in his partially inebriated state, Quinsy was touched. He was now a confidant of Dermot Bollinger, the millionaire owner of Serenity Quays.

"Do you understand the consequences of global warming, Quinsy?" Bollinger asked, as he swirled the remaining cognac around in the glass before he drank it.

Quinsy was confused. What sort of dumb arse question was that? he asked himself, as he tried to retain his sobriety and respond intelligently.

He was spared the embarrassment as Bollinger continued. "Did you know, Quinsy, that most of the land around Serenity Quays was originally a swamp that sits three metres below sea level?"

Quinsy shrugged. "Sure," he said, and drank the remainder of his cognac. Everyone at Serenity Quays knew its history, and how the developer had drained the swamp and created eighty-five building blocks along a series of canals.

Bollinger got to his feet and stood looking out the window across the water. Muriel and Mrs. Bollinger had left the dining room, as Muriel was feeling unwell. Quinsy had heard her throwing up in the guest's bathroom situated on the other side of the house.

"How would you feel, Quinsy, if I told you a fifty year flood would see most homes in Serenity Quays go under water?" He turned suddenly and raised a finger in the air. "What if I told you a one hundred year flood would be over the roofs of every house on the estate?"

Quinsy studied Bollinger for a time, taking in what he had said. Then he laughed loudly. "That couldn't happen, Mr. Bollinger—not with the canals and the river levees..."

"Levees? There are no river levees, Quinsy. And as for the canals, they'd just carry the floodwaters into every house."

The tone of the discussion had begun to disturb Quinsy. "Couldn't you just build some levees, Mr. Bollinger?"

"Where do you suggest we start, Quinsy? There are at least a dozen creeks that run off the hills behind the estate that flood in heavy rain. Do we build levees along them all, as well as the river?" Bollinger shook his head. " No, Quinsy, that wouldn't be possible."

Quinsy moved restlessly in his chair. "But there hasn't been any problem for eight years."

That's because of the El Nino, Quinsy—drought. We've had very little heavy rain in the past ten years, but that's about to change. A long wet period's now predicted." Bollinger poured them each another wine.

Quinsy was becoming distressed. Why was Bollinger confiding in him about such a serious matter? He didn't want to be privy to such a catastrophic scenario. "Why won't the flood waters simply run into the river and out to sea?" he asked.

"Normally they would, Quinsy, but when you combine heavy rain with a king tide, the water has nowhere to go except back into the old swamplands—into Serenity Quays."

Quinsy was silent for a time. When he spoke, it was as if to dispel the fear that had begun to overwhelm him. "Maybe we'll be lucky. Not all areas are effected by floods."

"If global warming continues at its current rate, no one living in low-lying areas on the coast will be spared. And we are overdue for another one hundred-year flood. It's coming, Quinsy, and sooner rather than later, I believe."

Bollinger studied Quinsy as he sat fidgeting with his wine glass. He almost felt sorry for the pathetic little man whom he was setting up as part of his outrageous plan.

* * *

"If we were any further from the dance floor, our table would be in the middle of the frigging pool." The Major and his wife Jessie had just settled into their designated seat for the Saturday night entertainment.

"Watch your language," Jessie said, looking around to see if anyone had heard her husband's outburst. "Anyway, I'd prefer to be as far away as possible from Bollinger's mob."

"Look at them," the Major said. "They always organise the best two tables for themselves. They're the first ones served with a meal, they're closest to the band and the dance floor, and nearest the bar." He dumped his esky heavily on the floor near their table, further emphasising his hostility towards the other group. " Makes you want to puke," he said loudly.

"Forget about it," Jessie said. "Our group will be here shortly, so sit back and enjoy yourself—and pour me a scotch and soda. I intend to have fun tonight, even if you don't."

Saturday evening was party time at Serenity Quays, and several residents had formed an old time dance band. The 'Saturday Night Jive' in the clubrooms, as it was called, had become a popular social event. Because most residents usually ate their 'tea' around five in the afternoon, proceedings started early, with dinner served no later than six. By seven, things were really heating up, and the noise in the poorly constructed clubrooms was almost unbearable. Fortunately, most of the tenants had hearing problems, and with the numbing effect of excessive alcohol, no one seemed to care. The entertainment continued well into the night—often as late as ten o'clock.

Although the clubrooms were located in the centre of the resort, a number of residents preferred to drive their cars. After a heavy night of drinking, many residents were incapable of walking home. Consequently, accidents were a regular occurrence, and walking around the estate on a Saturday night was extremely dangerous. The swimming pool was also a hazardous place. Not from intoxicated drivers, but from several residents who, after a few hours of raucous celebration, had a craven urge to remove their clothes and go skinny-dipping. To the sober observer, the sight of a group of merry middle-aged and overweight residents

41

frolicking naked in the resort's swimming pool could be a fascinating and even disturbing encounter.

One particularly frightening experience did linger in the minds of many. Maggie Pugh, slightly more inebriated than usual, had slipped while in the process of undressing and fell backwards into the spa—her size 24 girdle entangled around her legs. The danger was not to Maggie, but to the five people already in the spa, who suffered an assortment of sprains, bruises, and severe shock when Maggie tumbled in on top of them.

Jessie was relieved when Gerry Curry and his wife Sue arrived with Tony and Evy Bloom. A short time later, Penelope Applebee joined them, making up the full complement for their table. Penelope was a widow in her late fifties and, according to rumour, had lots of money. She was an attractive woman who had worked for years in various stage shows, and in television. As a consequence, she was targeted every Saturday night by several of the single males in the resort. Penny, as her close friends called her, sought refuge with the Major's group and joined them at their table.

"Sorry I'm late," she said, settling into her chair and extracting one of her two bottles of bubbly. "I couldn't get away from that doofus next door to me. Willy Hogan insisted I join him and his piss-pot friends at their table." She passed her bottle of bubbly to Gerry Curry, who popped the cork for her. "Clarissa was right about that man. He's getting worse, the horny old bastard. She thinks he's on some sort of medication."

"Really—a horny medication? That sounds interesting," Jessie replied. She grinned at Sue and Evy, and nodded towards her husband.

"So how'd you get rid of him?" Gerry asked.

"Told him I couldn't sit with them because I'm now a *Category 4*," she said, and giggled.

"Did you know the *Category 1* boys organised a petition asking for me to be barred from going near Grimes' office?" the Major said.

"They can't do that," Tony said. "Who organised the petition?"

"Well, they did," the Major replied. "Naylor and his perverse little mate Bullpit were hawking it around during a booze-up at Spencer Scraggs' place during the week."

"You know, that guy Scraggs worries me," Evy Bloom said, looking in the direction of Scraggs' table. "He's always hovering in the background, offering legal opinion and legislative advice to Bollinger's mob."

"The pretentious old fart paid me a visit a few days ago and warned me to keep away from you lot," said Penny, taking a sip of her drink. "He said you were all troublemakers, making things difficult for the other tenants in the resort."

"That's harassment," Tony said.

"Don't worry, sweetie, I told him where to get off," Penny replied.

"Felicity Grimes says he's a retired solicitor," Evy said.

"That's not true," Gerry commented almost to himself.

All eyes turned to Gerry, who was pouring himself another red wine. "I did some checks on him recently. It appears he was working as a law clerk for a Gold Coast firm about fifteen years ago when he was offered a job in real estate..."

"Let me guess," the Major interrupted. "The person who offered him the job was Dermot Bollinger?"

"You're right, Major. Bollinger owned a real estate business at the time in partnership with a shonky Gold Coast property developer named Fiddlemore. Scraggs worked for Bollinger and his mate for about ten years. It seems the trio got caught pulling some sort of tax scam and they decided to split up."

An awkward silence descended on the group as they considered the seriousness of Gerry Curry's disclosure.

It was Evy who broke the silence. "I hear some of the ladies are planning a nude calendar," she said, anxious to change the subject.

"Give us a break, Evy, " Gerry mumbled. "We haven't eaten yet."

"Well, I think it's a great idea," Sue said, raising her glass. "Providing no one asks me to pose for it."

"We're looking for a Miss July, Sue, if you change your mind." It was Sissy Witherspoon who leant across from the next table.

"You obviously haven't seen her naked," Gerry said.

"Another remark like that and I *might* change my mind," Sue responded.

"I think it'd be great for business, Gerry," Jessie said. "Your business partner posing as Miss July on your own company calendar."

"I think they should pose naked together as Mr. and Mrs. July," the Major added.

Sissy chuckled. "Major, I think you've come up with a great idea for next year's calendar."

"This is all a bit weird, I've got to say. Do you have volunteers for every month?" Tony asked.

"More than enough. Some we rejected, of course," Sissy replied, rolling her eyes. "All we need to find is a Miss July—how about you, Evy?"

Evy flushed with embarrassment. "No way," she said.

"I will," Jessie said.

"Like bloody hell you will," the Major exclaimed.

"Hey, if I want to take my gear off and pose naked for their calendar, I will," Jessie said with a hint of aggression.

"Sorry, Jessie," Sissy replied. "Legally, we're obliged to obtain your partner's approval." She turned to Tony Bloom. "What's this I hear about Bollinger shutting down our golf course?"

"Seems it's more than a rumour, Sissy. Bollinger wants to build houses on the site. Will your ladies sign our petition opposing the closure?" Tony asked.

"Of course we'll sign it," Sissy replied. "But what we really want is your nomination for the Tenants' Committee. We need someone that's independent and sensible to represent the silent majority in this place."

Tony responded with a wink. "I intend to, Sissy, but keep it to yourself for the time being."

"Great, you'll get our group's full support," she said, easing herself back to her table.

Sissy looked around at the couples at her table. Only Agnes Hoskiss was on her own. Her husband Charlie had suddenly fallen ill and was unable to attend. Bloody good job, Sissy thought. The man was a boring old prude who criticised his wife incessantly. And Agnes was taking every advantage of his absence. Sissy smiled as she watched Agnes and the newfound freedom she was experiencing. Because of her naughty calendar suggestion, Agnes Hoskiss was now a celebrity, and the toast of Serenity Quays. But Sissy was becoming a little concerned for Agnes' wellbeing. It wasn't so much the effects of the wine she was drinking, but more that she was responding to the advances of that lecherous old bastard Moose Dart, who was sitting at an adjoining table.

* * *

Milly and Alma Allbright were waiting outside the office as Felicity Grimes drove her car into the garage. It was 10:30 on Saturday night, and Felicity was not pleased to see them. This was her time away from the residents that she was forced to live and work with all week. Felicity had been to the movies with a male friend she was dating. She didn't attend the dances or any of the other social functions with the residents. "Management should not intrude on the residents' fun and enjoyment," she would respond when invited to any of the functions. In reality, Felicity could think of nothing worse than joining a bunch of geriatrics in their social activities. Now the Allbright sisters were about to encroach on *her* privacy. Why had she refused to spend the night at her friend's place when he'd invited her to stay? she asked herself.

"We have a prowler," Milly blurted out as Felicity approached them.

"A Peeping Tom, to be precise," Alma added.

Felicity studied the two women briefly. They fascinated her. They were a very private couple that rarely mixed with the other residents. The sisters were in their mid sixties, and although they were alike in many ways, they differed markedly in stature. Milly Allbright was a small, frail woman, while her sister was tall and buxom.

"Are you sure it wasn't another resident just passing your house?" Felicity asked as she slipped the key into her front door.

"He was looking in our bathroom window while Alma was taking a shower," Milly replied in her pixie voice.

"Your bathroom window is too high for anyone to look through," Felicity said in an indifferent tone.

"He moved one of our potted plants to stand on," Alma replied loudly. "It's still there if you care to come and see."

"Did you see who it was?" Felicity asked, suddenly realising the seriousness of the sisters' claim.

"Not really," Alma said, "but I'll never forget those beady eyes looking at me through that window."

"I'm sure it's not what it seems, ladies. Leave it with me and I'll make some inquiries tomorrow morning," Felicity said as she opened her door. The women were beginning to annoy her—their story was obviously a figment of their demented imaginations, she thought.

The two women did not move. "That's not good enough, Felicity," Alma said. "We want you to call the police."

Felicity stopped in the doorway and turned to face them. "The police?"

"Yes, the police. And we want you to call them tonight," Milly said, placing her hands defiantly on her hips.

Chapter Seven

Charlie Hoskiss clenched his fist and pounded on the office door, shattering the silence that prevailed around Serenity Quays early on Sunday morning. He waited a moment, and when there was no response, he banged loudly on the door once again. A light appeared from inside the house and Felicity Grimes responded angrily. "All right, I'm coming."

The door opened slightly and Felicity peered out into the early morning gloom. "Mr. Hoskiss," she said, rubbing her eyes, "what's wrong?"

"Agnes didn't come home from the dance last night," he replied. "Where is she?"

Felicity wrapped her gown around her, and then opened the door a little wider. She was exhausted. The police hadn't left until well after midnight, and now Charlie Hoskiss was banging on her door at five-thirty in the morning wanting to know where his wife was. The world's gone mad, she said to herself.

She quickly ushered Hoskiss into her lounge room, then went to the kitchen and switched on the kettle. "Now, Mr. Hoskiss, do you mind telling me why you've woken me at this hour? Your wife's personal affairs are not really my problem."

"Affairs?" Hoskiss shouted indignantly. "My wife isn't having any affairs, Ms. Grimes. She's missing, possibly kidnapped, or lying injured somewhere."

Felicity watched Charlie Hoskiss as he paced the floor while she made them a cup of tea. He may be a grumpy old bastard, she thought, but he seemed genuinely concerned about his wife.

"Your wife stayed on at the dance after you left, Mr. Hoskiss?"

"Agnes went to the dance on her own. I told her not to go, but she ignored me. The woman's a fool," he said. "The way she's been behaving lately—that ridiculous calendar, for instance."

"Everyone seems to think the calendar is a great idea, Mr. Hoskiss. You should be proud of your wife for suggesting it."

"Proud of what, Ms. Grimes? The woman is out of control—and the damage her wanton behaviour is doing to my good name..."

I was wrong, Felicity thought. The man is more concerned about his own reputation than his wife's wellbeing. "Whose table was she at?" she asked.

"We usually sit with the Witherspoons."

Felicity Grimes picked up the phone and began dialling the number. She didn't like Sissy Witherspoon. She was a borderline *Category 3*, and questioned many decisions management made. Now she was about to ring her early on a Sunday morning—the woman wouldn't be impressed. But Agnes Hoskiss was at her table, so this was her problem. And besides, she needed to get Charlie Hoskiss out of her house so she could get some sleep.

"Agnes is not my responsibility, Felicity," Sissy commented after Felicity had explained the reason for Charlie Hoskiss' anxiety. "If Mr. Hoskiss is that concerned, maybe you should call the police."

Christ, call in the police again? Felicity thought. No bloody way.

"Did you see Agnes leave?" Felicity asked, ignoring Sissy's suggestion.

"Not really. She was circulating around the tables towards the end of the evening. She was pretty tipsy, though. Everyone was filling her glass and toasting her."

"So you didn't see her leave with anyone?" Felicity asked.

Sissy hesitated. "No, but I was a little concerned about that man, Michael Dart. He seemed to be paying Agnes a lot of attention during the night."

Felicity gasped. "Moose Dart?" she said loudly.

"What about Moose Dart?" shouted Charlie, who had been sitting drinking his tea and listening to the one-sided conversation. He was now on his feet.

Felicity quickly terminated the call with Sissy Witherspoon as Charlie disappeared through her door, heading off in the direction of Moose Dart's house. Felicity was in a quandary. She was still in her nightie and dressing gown, but she needed to follow Hoskiss and prevent any likely trouble. She grabbed her slippers, then took off down the road, calling Charlie to wait for her. When she reached the Dart house, Charlie was already banging on the door. A moment later, a bleary eyed Moose Dart stood glaring angrily in his doorway, naked except for a towel wrapped around his waist.

"What the fuck...?" Moose shouted at Charlie.

"Where's my wife?" he demanded.

"Your wife?" Moose turned towards his bedroom. "She's not your wife."

As he turned back towards his intruder, Charlie Hoskiss swung a punch that landed flush on Moose's face, sending him sprawling on the floor. Hoskiss stepped past him, heading towards the bedroom.

As Felicity stepped through the doorway, she was struck with delight and fascination. Moose Dart lay sprawled on the floor, his discarded bath towel lying a short distance away. Felicity stared, transfixed by Dart's majestic manhood that still stood proudly between his legs, despite the man's semi conscious condition. It was a woman's piercing scream that forced Felicity Grimes to avert her gaze from the naked man at her feet. As she moved towards the bedroom, Charlie Hoskiss brushed past her, mumbling angrily to himself, and disappeared through the door. Felicity looked in the bedroom and stared opened mouthed at the woman sitting on the bed. It was Dolly Mott.

"I was hiding under the sheet, and he pulled it off me—he saw me naked," Dolly cried pitifully.

* * *

"What were the police doing here last night?" Gerry Curry asked, as he watched his golf ball land within two metres of the hole.

"Probably came to arrest Felicity Grimes for being a public nuisance," the Major replied in a cynical tone.

Tony Bloom selected a ball from the bucket that sat to one side on the elevated tee. "My sources tell me we have a voyeur loose in the resort."

"You're kidding?" Gerry said, then grinned broadly. "A Peeping Tom in Serenity Quays? The poor bastard must be hard up—excuse the expression—if he gets his jollies in this place."

"Who was the lucky victim?" the Major asked.

"The Allbright sisters," Tony replied. "Caught him perving on one of them in the shower."

"Unbelievable," Gerry said.

The three men continued hitting balls to the green until the bucket was empty. This was a regular routine for them every Sunday morning. They would share a bucket of practice balls on the 165-metre, single-hole golf course, then spend several hours on maintenance work.

"One of my balls went over to the left in those trees," Gerry remarked, breaking from the other two as they approached the green. Gerry ventured into the bushes where he thought the ball had landed. It was a cluster of mature bottlebrush with a covering of light rough beneath the overhanging branches. Gerry was pulling back several branches with his club as he searched for the wayward ball, when he stepped back in alarm.

"Hey fellers, you'd better come over here and see this."

A short time later, the three men stood staring in disbelief at Agnes Hoskiss, who lay propped up against one of the small trees. Her head was slumped on her chest—in one hand was an empty bottle of pink champagne, and in the other, a wine glass.

"Is she dead?" the Major asked.

Gerry bent down and checked Agnes' breathing. As he did so, she opened her eyes and looked up at him. She smiled and placed the palm of her hand on his chest. "No Gerry," she said in a strange husky voice, "you're a very attractive man, and I'd love you to kiss me, but you're married—it wouldn't be right."

Agnes looked past Gerry and saw the amused faces of the other two men looking down at her. She struggled to her feet and immediately fell into Gerry's arms. He caught her, then helped her out onto the fairway. After a moment, she was able to stand without too much assistance, and began brushing down her clothes. To the men's surprise, the usually shy and conservative Agnes Hoskiss did not seem the least bit embarrassed by her predicament.

"I got lost on the way home from the dance last night," she giggled, placing her hand over her mouth. "I must've fallen asleep under that tree."

Gerry was still holding her for fear she would topple back into her resting-place. "Are you okay?" he asked.

"I think someone put something in my drink, but I'm fine now." She smiled at them. "I'd best get home or Charlie will be worried." She bent down and removed her shoes, then turned and slowly, and a little unsteadily, made her way across the fairway. She had gone a short distance when she called back to the three men who hadn't moved. "You won't mention to anyone how you found me, will you?"

They shook their heads and watched her until she had disappeared from sight.

"The woman's demented," Tony commented after she had gone.

"Why do you say that?" the Major asked.

"Anyone who thinks Gerry Curry is an attractive man has completely lost their marbles."

* * *

Sunday was proving to be quite relaxing for Quinsy and Muriel as they ate breakfast on Bollinger's boat, which was anchored in the waterway a short distance from the house. A planned day's fishing was cancelled, as Quinsy and Muriel weren't feeling all that well.

"I think we have the numbers to close down the golf course," Quinsy remarked, as he sipped his second cup of coffee.

"We may put those plans on hold for the present," Bollinger replied. "In light of last night's discussion, we can't risk building any more homes on the estate."

"Homes? I thought you were turning the golfing area into open parkland?" Quinsy responded.

Bollinger moved uncomfortably in his deck chair, aware of his awkward slip-up. "Homes, parklands—any new facilities in the resort." Bollinger leant forward and touched Quinsy's knee. "You do understand the seriousness of our discussion last night, don't you, Quinsy?"

Quinsy was still coming to terms with the discussion of the previous evening, but Bollinger's intimate touching gesture moved him.

"Yes, sir," he replied. "I understand."

Bollinger sat back in his chair and lit a cigar. "How would you and Muriel like to move to our new resort on the Tweed Coast?"

"Hideaway Cove?" Quinsy's voice rose. Even Muriel, suffering the effects of a serious hangover, suddenly became interested in the conversation.

"Yes, to a new section in the resort that we're opening shortly."

Everyone at Serenity Quays knew of Hideaway Cove, and many were envious of the residents who lived there. It was close to the beach, had a nine-hole golf course, a large bowling green, and it was only fifteen minutes drive from the Gold Coast.

"Aren't you having a problem with that development?" Quinsy asked.

Bollinger's *problem* had made the national news. The Department of Land and Environment had ruled that the area he was planning to develop was pristine native habitat and subject to strict development guidelines, but Bollinger went ahead and cleared the land anyway.

"Bunch of tree hugging left-wing greenies standing in the way of progress," Bollinger shouted. "It's too late for them to do anything now; the first twenty blocks will be available for occupancy in two weeks." Bollinger leant forward. "These will be the best blocks, Quinsy, nearest the beach, brand new homes, and you and Muriel can have first choice."

Quinsy was wary. "What about my moving costs?"

"Because of your, um…special relationship with our company, we'd pay for your relocation costs. Obviously that would need to remain confidential." Bollinger sat back and drew on his cigar. "Naturally, we couldn't do that for the other eighty-four home owners."

Quinsy looked stunned. "You intend to move everyone out of Serenity Quays?"

"Of course," Bollinger replied, with an exaggerated look of surprise. "You did say you understood the serious nature of the situation there, didn't you, Quinsy?"

"Yes, but you're going to move every tenant out of Serenity Quays to Hideaway Cove?"

Bollinger spread his arms in a welcoming gesture. "Everyone who wants to come."

"Jesus, that'll cost you a fortune."

Bollinger got to his feet and stood by the boat's railing, looking out across the water. "I'm a tough businessman, Quinsy," he said, blowing a smoke ring in the air, "but I've always maintained a policy of decency and integrity in my business affairs. There are times, Quinsy, when one has to make difficult decisions, moral decisions that have nothing to do with money or success. They're judgements that relate to one's responsibilities and duty towards those people who are in his care—like all my tenants at Serenity Quays." Bollinger moved from the handrail and stood behind Muriel, his hand resting on the back of her chair. "Quinsy, such decisions can place a person in my position in serious jeopardy." He sighed heavily and returned to the boat railing. "People may see my generosity as a weakness or a frailty, and they could try to take advantage of this situation."

Despite the fact that Muriel had little idea what Bollinger was alluding to, she was unable to contain her emotions and began to weep. Quinsy was also confused, but nodded vigorously, hoping that his enthusiasm would indicate to Bollinger his deep and total understanding of whatever the man was prattling on about.

"It's very important, Quinsy, that the push to have everyone move from Serenity Quays to Hideaway Cove has the full support and backing of the Tenants' Committee."

Quinsy opened his mouth to reply, but he was checked by Bollinger's raised hand.

"But what's more important is that we don't cause a panic and alert the press. The last thing we need is bad publicity about this move." Bollinger sat down in front of Quinsy once again. "We need to get our message through to all the tenants, Quinsy." He stubbed his cigar in the ashtray. "This is an outstanding investment opportunity for everyone in Serenity Quays, and a chance to improve their lifestyle dramatically."

"I agree, Mr. Bollinger, but how much is it going to cost the tenants?"

"We plan to offer each tenant at Serenity Quays the opportunity to take up a block in a comparable style of home at Hideaway Cove for an all up price of six thousand dollars."

"Will that include their removal costs?" Quinsy asked.

"Everything, including accommodation in a motel if a tenant's house isn't completed when they move."

Quinsy glanced at Muriel. "That's very fair, Mr. Bollinger, but what if the tenant doesn't have that sort of money?"

"They can pay it off over the next five years—we'll add it to their weekly rent." Bollinger cleared his throat. "There'd be a small interest charge in that situation, of course."

"Of course," Quinsy replied, and cleared his throat as well, as if to acknowledge some hidden meaning in the gesture. "But what if a tenant doesn't want to go to Hideaway Cove?"

"For the same amount, we'll move their house to another park if they wish, providing it's within one hundred kilometres. Any further and there'll be an additional mileage charge, naturally."

"Naturally," Quinsy repeated. "But what if they don't want to leave Serenity Quays? Some of the tenants have family in the area."

"They can stay in the area if they choose, but you must understand, Quinsy, we'll be closing Serenity Quays. We're not renewing any more leases."

Quinsy looked at his wife with alarm. His mouth was dry, and he swallowed noisily. Finally, Quinsy Naylor realised the enormity of the task Dermot Bollinger had set before him.

Chapter Eight

Lily Hartmann dropped the six bags of heavy groceries on her kitchen bench, then flexed her shoulders. Lily was remarkably fit for someone her age, and extremely strong for a woman—a consequence, her late husband would argue, of serving twenty years in the Israeli army.

It had been a busy day for Lily. She had driven to Lismore to visit her husband's grave, and then gone shopping. Lily generally avoided leaving Sammy alone for long periods, as he became agitated, and would screech and swear loudly until she returned. When Lily arrived home, Sammy's behaviour would change dramatically. He would become quiet and moody, and ignore her for hours. That was the bird's way of showing his disapproval at being left alone. Sammy's reaction to her absence disturbed Lily somewhat, because her dead husband had behaved in exactly the same way.

"G'day, cocky," she said. She always used her dead husband's greeting. "You angry with Lily, uh?" she added, as she began putting her frozen items in the freezer.

She glanced at the large white bird, with its plumed head feathers, perched in his cage that swung from a wrought iron stand on her back verandah. The bird's steely black eyes were fixed on Lily as she moved around the kitchen.

"Visited our old mate today, Sammy. Told him they want to throw us out." She glanced at the bird once again. "You know what he said to me, Sammy?" She chuckled when she remembered her Aussie husband's favourite expression. "Tell 'em all to get fucked."

Lily stored the last of the groceries, then began to fix Sammy his favourite treat—vegemite on fresh bread and butter. "This make Sammy talk to mummy again," she said as she opened the cage. As she did so, the bird toppled forward into her arms.

A few moments later, a loud piercing scream was clearly heard by everyone in Serenity Quays.

* * *

"The bird was dead in its cage?" the Major asked.

"Stiff as a board, sitting slumped on its perch," Tony replied. The two men were enjoying a beer on the Major's verandah.

"And they're saying the bird was poisoned?" The Major was fascinated by the story.

"Apparently so. It appears someone fed the bird a large dose of human prescription medication, and it had a violent reaction. Probably died instantly from a massive heart attack."

"What sort of medication—do they know?"

"The police found several foil tablet wrappers in the bottom of the cage. It was a drug called Cialis."

"What's that?"

"It's a sex enhancement drug for men, something like Viagra."

"Why would anyone do that?" The Major was having difficulty hiding his amusement.

"Some sort of prank, I guess, or maybe someone with a grudge."

"You don't hold grudges against Lily Hartmann," the major responded, "unless you have a death wish. I hear she spent most of her life in the Israeli army."

Tony laughed. "Well, there are plenty of suspects; the bird was becoming a real nuisance."

"What does Ms. Grimes plan to do about it?" the Major asked.

"Absolutely nothing. Someone even suggested that she could have been responsible."

"What would Felicity Grimes be doing with a male sex drug?" The major hesitated, then coughed. "No, let's not go down that road," he said. "So who do you think is responsible?"

"It could have been anyone, I guess. Seems half the men in the resort are taking this, Cialis. The word is someone in Serenity Quays is doing a roaring trade selling the stuff."

"You're kidding—that's illegal," the Major said. "Do you know who?"

Tony grinned. "Would you believe Moose Dart?"

"Why am I not surprised," the Major replied.

* * *

Most afternoons, a select group of male tenants met in the resort's sports room. The sports room was an ugly building that jutted off the main clubrooms like a large appendage. It had been built with a special grant from Bollinger as a meeting place for the men of Serenity Quays to get together, have a few drinks, and behave like normal blokes.

There was little sporting equipment in the room apart from a mini pool table, a dartboard, and an area for carpet bowls. The main purpose of the facility was not for sport, however. It was a safe and comfortable environment where the men could get away from their women for a few hours. Most afternoons the men sat around telling dirty jokes, or putting down those tenants not interested in sharing the group's unsocial and boorish behaviour.

There were a number of restrictions as to who participated in the group's activities. There were definitely no women allowed, although special dispensation was given to Lily Hartmann, who could drink, swear, and tell dirty yarns as well as any of the men. People like Maurice and Benny were barred, as were all *Category*

60

4 tenants. Quinsy Naylor and his mate Arty Bullpit strictly controlled attendances at the sports club—and while interlopers were not asked to leave, they were made to feel so uncomfortable during their first visit that they rarely returned.

It was 5:30 in the afternoon, and the table was liberally scattered with empty bottles of home brew and other assorted alcoholic beverages. Pool, darts, and carpet bowls had long been abandoned for the men's preferred sporting activity—serious drinking.

"Are you going to tell us how you got that black eye, Moose?" Gill Trotter asked.

"I walked into a door," Moose answered.

Trotter gave a raucous laugh. "That's not what I heard," he said.

Moose's face flushed red. "What *did* you hear, smart arse?"

"That Charlie Hoskiss caught you bonking his wife," Quinsy Naylor commented from the next table.

"That's bullshit. I hardly know his wife," Moose replied, as he poured himself another drink.

Arty Bullpit held up his glass of home brew and admired its consistency in the light. "Well, the story goes that he caught you humping someone this morning," he said.

"If you must know," Moose said, glaring at Bullpit, "Hoskiss burst into my house early this morning and king hit me. He claimed his wife was in my bed. The stupid idiot frightened the bejesus out of Dolly."

A hush descended over the room.

It was Marty Fisk who broke the silence. "You're sleeping with Dolly Mott?"

"She's a widow—why not?" Moose replied.

"Jesus, Moose," Gill Trotter mumbled. "Those bloody Viagra tablets of yours are gonna land you in big trouble one day."

There was a murmur of agreement around the room.

"What's this story about a Peeping Tom?" Arty Bullpit asked.

"Someone was caught watching one of the Allbright sisters taking a shower on Saturday night," Marty Fisk replied.

"What sort of wacko would want to perve on those two old biddies?" Quinsy Naylor asked.

"Particularly the big one—she's as ugly as sin," Clarry Humphries scoffed.

"She's not a woman, she's a man."

All eyes turned to Harry Smutzig, who was sitting at a table on his own, slumped over a bottle of bourbon.

"How do you know that?" Willy Hogan asked.

Harry took another drink of the almost empty bottle in front of him. "Because I saw her…er, him, in da shower."

Moose Dart sniggered. "So you're the Peeping Tom?" he said.

"Ya, and dis is your bloody fault, Moose," Harry slurred. "It was dose bloody sex tablets you sold me—dey made me go all randy."

* * *

Felicity Grimes slumped back into her chair in disbelief. "A police drug raid? That can't be possible!" she said to the senior police officer holding the search warrant out for her inspection. "Not here, not at Serenity Quays."

"I'm afraid so, Madam. Now, if you would kindly give me the security code for the gates so my men can carry out our search warrants," he said. The plain-clothes Federal Police officer spoke with the disciplined authority of someone who had conducted numerous drug raids.

Felicity managed to scribble the code number on a scrap of paper, then handed it to the policeman. "Can I inquire as to whose

property you plan to search, officer?" she asked, as she struggled
to regain her composure.

"I'm sorry, I can't answer that." He studied the code, and
then returned the paper to her. "Are there any other exits from the
resort, Madam?" he asked, looking at the large aerial map of
Serenity Quays on the wall.

"Only these two pedestrian gates," she said, and pointed to
the locations.

"We'll be placing officers on each of the exits. No one is to
leave the resort during our search. And please, don't phone anyone
until I say so. Do you understand, Ms. Grimes?"

"My boss, I'll have to ring my boss," she pleaded.

"No one, Ms. Grimes—not even your boss. It shouldn't take
us long to conduct our investigations here." He hurried from the
office, then slipped into the first of two cars containing a number
of plain clothed officers.

Felicity stood watching as the security gates closed behind
the two vehicles. One of policemen alighted from the second
vehicle before it moved off, and he took up a position inside the
exit gate. Felicity was finding it difficult to comprehend what had
just occurred. One of her tenants—a drug dealer! If this leaked out
to the media, all her hard work building up the resort's image
would be destroyed.

For the next ten minutes, Felicity sat at her desk, unsure of
what she should do next. She was concerned that Bollinger might
blame her for not maintaining stricter control within the resort, and
would hold her responsible for any bad publicity that could result
from this unpleasant incident. And what if someone rang Dermot
and told him what had occurred? There were a number of people
who would love to embarrass her, and would go running to her
boss with half the facts.

Stuff the Federal Police, she thought. Dermot needs to know.
She had just picked up the phone and begun dialling his number

when she saw the two police cars exiting the resort. She got to her feet and rushed to the window in time to see a handcuffed civilian wedged between two burly police officers in the second vehicle. She stared in shocked disbelief as the vehicle sped away. They had arrested Moose Dart!

Felicity picked up the phone and began dialling Bollinger's number again. She had her back to the window and didn't see the police vehicle pull in beside her office. She turned with a start as someone behind her cleared his throat. Felicity stared at her unexpected visitor, unable to move, the telephone in her hand hanging limply by her side.

Bollinger answered the phone. "Hello," he said several times, but Felicity did not respond. Instead she hung up.

"Yes?" Felicity said when she was finally able to speak.

"I'm sorry to bother you, Ms. Grimes," the uniformed policeman said, holding up a formal document. "We've had a report of a home invasion and an assault on two of your tenants. Could you direct me to the residence of a Charlie Hoskiss?"

* * *

Felicity sat hunched over her desk, staring at the phone. The need to ring Dermot Bollinger was no longer a priority. Now she was terrified that *he* would ring her before she had an explanation for the weird events that were occurring around her. The Federal Police were saying nothing, and she had no idea where they had taken Moose Dart. She had rung Quinsy Naylor, but all he could say was that Moose was arrested for selling some sort of sex drug to the other tenants. And now the local police had arrived to investigate the incident on Sunday morning involving Charlie Hoskiss and Moose Dart. But where were they? They had gone to interview Charlie over an hour ago and hadn't returned.

Felicity looked up as the gates opened and the police car emerged. It sped past her window without stopping. She caught a glimpse of someone sitting in the back of the vehicle, but it wasn't Charlie Hoskiss—it looked like Harry Smutzig.

The phone rang five times before she raised the courage to pick it up. "Hello," she said in a hushed voice.

"It's Milly here, Felicity, Milly Allbright. They got our Peeping Tom. It was Harry Smutzig. He admitted everything."

Felicity was unable to respond for a moment as she tried to take in what Milly Allbright had said.

"That's nice, Milly," she eventually replied in a monotone voice. "Thank you for letting me know."

Felicity replaced the receiver, then went to the lower drawer of her filing cabinet where she removed an unopened bottle of Black Label Johnny Walker whisky. It had been a Christmas present from one of the tenants. She took a paper cup from the water cooler and filled it with the amber liquid. She locked her office door, closed the blinds, and took the phone off the hook. Felicity Grimes did not want to be disturbed for the rest of the day.

* * *

Stanley Bancroft was watching the home of his neighbour, Roberto DeAngelo, as he washed his dishes. Stanley had offered to visit Roberto while he was in hospital, but Ricky had warned against it, much to Stanley's relief.

Now the old man had been released from hospital and had returned to Serenity Quays. Stanley knew he was home because he could see the lights on inside the house. How, Stanley asked himself, could they send the man home so soon? He was severely depressed, and with suicidal tendencies. Now *he*, Stanley Bancroft, was going to be held responsible for the man's wellbeing. The call had come from Ricky DeAngelo earlier in the day. He rang to say that now that Ricky and he were brothers, Roberto DeAngelo was Stanley's Poppa too, so he would leave him in his trusted care.

Stanley heard a noise and looked out into DeAngelo's carport. Through the lattice, he could make out Mr. DeAngelo, who appeared to be standing on the bonnet of his small car. Then Stanley stared in amazement. The old man seemed to be walking—he was walking in mid air.

Stanley dropped the plate he was washing and it smashed to the floor in small pieces. He ran from his kitchen across his patio towards Mr. DeAngelo's carport. As he turned the corner of the house, Stanley was shocked by what he saw. Acting quickly, he grabbed Mr. DeAngelo's legs, taking the full weight of his body despite being kicked and punched about the head by the old man.

"Help me, Maurice!" he screamed frantically. "Help me, Benny!"

Stanley wasn't sure how long he supported Mr. DeAngelo before help arrived, but he was close to exhaustion when he saw Maurice leap onto the car and release the rope from around the old man's neck. When he did, the two men fell to the ground in a tangled heap—Mr. DeAngelo's face almost touching Stanley's.

"I kill you," DeAngelo rasped hoarsely before he fell into unconsciousness.

Chapter Nine

Evy Bloom was unsure whether to take Badminton-Smyth's comment seriously. "Are you certain these people were negotiating to buy a house in Serenity Quays?" she asked.

"Most definitely," Badminton-Smyth replied. They mentioned lot twenty-seven, and Felicity had asked them to come into the office so they could discuss the sale."

"I think you'd better come and hear this," Tony called to Gerry, who had just arrived at the Bloom's house. "It looks like we're getting some bikies in the resort."

"Bikies—you must be joking," Gerry replied.

"I was there on Friday when the man and his woman called into Felicity's office. Nasty types they were, with tattoos on their arms and metal studs on their faces." Badminton-Smyth shuddered. "And the bike had those high-rise handlebars, and the noise it made was deafening."

"Yeah, I heard it leave the resort; it sounded like a low flying jet," Tony remarked.

"They both had grubby leather jackets with *Bikies from Hell* printed on the back." There was a look of indignation on Badminton-Smyth's face. "The man was very aggressive—he threatened me."

"Maybe Felicity was just going through the motions, Charles. She may have been scared to turn them away," Gerry suggested.

"And Grimes has final say as to who buys into Serenity Quays. There's *no way* she'd allow a sale to the type of person you've described," Tony added.

"Well, I heard Felicity say their offer to purchase number twenty-seven had been accepted." Badminton-Smyth became thoughtful for a moment. "But then this morning I saw them inspecting the Dumbelton house behind me," he added.

"Maybe Elsie Parker didn't want to sell her house to bikies," Gerry said.

"Elsie doesn't give a damn who buys her house, she just wants to get out of Serenity Quays," Evy said.

Gerry turned to Badminton-Smyth. "Why did the man threaten you?"

Badminton-Smyth shrugged. "I just made a comment to Felicity that they weren't the type of resident we wanted in Serenity Quays." He looked up to see a bewildered expression on Tony's face. "As a resident of Serenity Quays, I'm entitled to speak my mind."

Tony shook his head in disbelief. "Not in front of a *Bikies from Hell* member, you're not," he said.

"Have you spoken with Quinsy Naylor?" Gerry asked. "The Tenants' Committee can demand that the sale does not proceed."

"Naylor has notified Grimes that the committee has no objection to these people buying into the resort," Badminton-Smyth replied.

"Why would they do that? Gerry asked. "Even Bollinger's mob wouldn't want a bikie gang member living near them."

"There's some really weird things happening around this place lately," Sue said, looking thoughtful. "Like those men we saw in the resort this morning. Who do you think *they* were?"

Evy laughed. "They looked like FBI agents," she said.

"Probably the Mafia, if they were friends of Bollingers," Gerry said.

"Have you heard that the removal of our golf course is no longer on the agenda?" Tony commented.

"No, who told you that?" Gerry asked.

"Felicity rang me an hour ago. She said Bollinger wasn't going to build any more homes in Serenity Quays, so the driving range can stay." Tony unfolded a sheet of paper. "We've also discovered that leases on this list of homes have not been submitted to the authorities for renewal," he said, and placed the sheet of paper on the table.

"What in God's name is Bollinger up to?" Evy asked.

Gerry Curry was about to offer an explanation, then he hesitated. His appointment in the morning with a Gold Coast property developer would confirm the rumours he was hearing about the sale of Serenity Quays. If the reports were correct, it would explain some of Bollinger's recent actions.

There was no sense in alarming his friends now, he decided. He would wait until after the meeting to reveal his disturbing piece of information.

* * *

"This is only the first photo shoot ladies," Hamish MacTaggit shouted loudly. "The three summer girls are the only people we need today."

They had been going less than an hour, and the young photographer had already seen enough to alarm him. Some of the loud and boisterous women that now surrounded his work area seemed more ancient than his own grandmother. The thought of having to work with these women for the next two weeks, and be forced to observe their nakedness—even their most intimate parts—was a terrifying prospect for the young man.

There were a large number of onlookers, including several pernicious looking men, lurking around the building. One, he noticed, even had a camera.

"I must ask everyone other than the December, January, and February models to leave the building," MacTaggit called loudly.

There was a brief lull in the noise, then it began again, louder than before. MacTaggit looked on in desperation—his plea had been ignored.

"You heard the photographer," Sissy Witherspoon shouted from somewhere in the midst of the crowd. "Everyone not required here today, please leave."

MacTaggit retreated to the set that was being organised for the December shoot. As he watched the two people who had volunteered to prepare his miniature beach scene, he was captivated. What they had created was outstanding. The taller of the two men saw him observing their work and approached him. He was in his early sixties, slim, and seemingly very fit. He wore pale yellow jodhpurs and a matching silk shirt.

He stood alongside MacTaggit for a moment, one hand on his hip and the other poised delicately under his chin. "My little man is just a genius, don't you think, duckie?" Maurice asked proudly, as they watched Benny at work.

MacTaggit turned to the man standing beside him. To his knowledge, he had never worked this closely with homosexuals before, and he was fascinated. It had never occurred to him that older men would live together in such a relationship, and certainly not at Serenity Quays.

"What you've done with the backdrop is wonderful," MacTaggit said, and sighed. "Maybe you two will bring some sanity into this whole ridiculous fiasco."

"Oh, don't be too hard on the ladies, duckie," Maurice said, waving a cupped hand at the now departing crowd of women. "This calendar's the most exciting thing that's happened to the old dears in years."

* * *

Felicity looked up from her desk and glared at the person standing in front of her. "Shit, what now?" she asked.

"There's been another assault reported, Ms. Grimes." The policeman grinned at her. "Your resort is becoming a regular battleground," he said.

Felicity scowled at the policeman, as if he were the felon. "Who this time?" she asked in an abrupt tone of voice.

The policeman's manner became a little more serious. "A Mrs. Fisk rang the station this morning. She said her husband had been badly bashed."

"Marty Fisk—who'd bother assaulting him?" she mumbled as she and the policeman set off towards the Fisk's residence. Felicity had decided she would sit in on any police investigations in future.

Felicity was becoming immune to the many strange developments within her once quiet and respectable resort. Nothing surprised her anymore. Of all the recent incidents, the police were only interested in Moose Dart's drug distribution business. The Allbright sisters had dropped their complaint against Harry Smutzig when Harry announced that he was selling out and going back to Germany. The police decided not to pursue the matter when they discovered that one of the sisters was, in fact, a brother in drag. It still remained a mystery to Felicity why Harry, a 73-year bachelor, had any use for a sex enhancement drug. Assault charges against Charlie Hoskiss by Dolly Mott were also considered trivial, and Moose Dart had enough problems to worry about without pursuing the black eye he'd received from Charlie.

When they first arrived at the house, Marty Fisk refused to be interviewed, remaining in his room for some time before his wife was able to coax him out. It was obvious that Marty was angry that the police had become involved in the incident.

"You were home on your own when the assault occurred?" the policeman asked.

"Yes he was," Jo Jo Fisk replied. "I found him lying on the floor when I got back from shopping."

The policeman glared at Jo Jo. "I'd like your husband to answer my questions if you don't mind, Madam."

Marty patted his injured face. He had a black eye, a bloody nose, and a badly swollen lip.

The policeman sighed. He was not happy the way the interview was going, and his impatience was beginning to show. "I'll ask you again, Mr. Fisk. Did you recognise the person or persons who assaulted you?"

"No. I was mixing some home brew in the laundry when they came up behind me," Marty replied.

Jo Jo glared at her husband. "If they attacked you from behind, how come you've got so many injuries to your face?" she asked.

The police officer glared at Jo Jo again. "Look, Mr. Fisk, if you want us to take your claim seriously, you'll need to give us some specific information. We need some details to work on. How many men were there, their description, skin and hair colouring—anything?"

Marty glanced at his wife. "There was only one, a big guy, black hair—and yeah, he had a dark complexion, but I didn't get a good look because he hit me from behind."

"Dark complexion you say, how dark? An aborigine, an Indian, an African maybe? Come on, Mr. Fisk, I think you're making this up as you go along. Did you, or did you not, recognise the person who assaulted you?" By now the police officer was ready to terminate the interview.

"I told you," Marty said, getting up from his chair and taking a pack of aspirin from one of the kitchen cupboards. "I was struck from behind."

The police officer shook his head. "Struck with what, Mr. Fisk?"

"A fist—she king hit me," Fisk mumbled.

"She—did a woman assault you, Mr. Fisk?" The policeman turned to Jo Jo.

"Don't look at me," Jo Jo said with a shrug. "I didn't touch him."

"Did you know the woman, Mr. Fisk?" the policeman asked.

"What woman?" Marty looked nervous. "It was a big guy, with dark skin."

"You said *she* king hit you," Felicity Grimes remarked.

"No I didn't," Marty argued.

"Yes you bloody did," Jo Jo shouted.

Marty Fisk looked around the room; he felt trapped. He had taken six aspirin, but his head still ached and his right eye was closing rapidly. And Marty was losing control. He was feeling ill and needed urgent medical treatment, so why were all theses people harassing him? He placed his face in his hands and slumped back into the lounge chair.

Felicity Grimes came and stood in front of him. "It was Lily Hartmann who beat you up, wasn't it, Marty?"

Marty Fisk lowered his head and began to weep. The embarrassment was too much for him. After he had regained his composure, he spoke without looking up. "She came in here this morning and accused me of killing her cockatoo. She called me a murderer, so I went to throw her out, and when I grabbed her, she whacked me in the face."

"I told you not to give those Viagra tablets to that bird," Jo Jo said, shaking her fist angrily at her husband. "You're a bloody idiot, Marty."

"It was a joke. We didn't think it'd die."

The policeman stared at Marty, a look of disbelief on his face. "You fed her bird a sex enhancement drug?" he asked.

"It was just a joke," Marty repeated.

The policeman turned to Felicity as he placed his notebook in his pocket. "This looks like an internal problem to me, Ms. Grimes—I'll leave it to you to sort out."

* * *

Stanley Bancroft was not surprised to receive another visit from Ricky DeAngelo. Ricky had come to pay his respects following the incident in Roberto's carport. When the hugging and kissing had finished, he held Stanley by the shoulders.

"Hey, what can I say, Bancroft, you're one of them—what does Father Mulligan call 'em? A guardian angel, that's what you are, Bancroft, a fuckin' guardian angel."

He handed him the regulation bunch of flowers, then sat in Stanley's favourite leather lounge chair. His two cronies stood each side of the front door, one holding a metal briefcase.

Stanley selected a vase and began arranging the flowers.

"Get your old lady to do that, I wanna talk," DeAngelo said abruptly.

Stanley continued with the flower arrangement. "I don't have an old...a lady, but I do enjoy working with flowers."

There was a look of concern on DeAngelo's face. "You ain't one of those *backwards boys,* are ya Bancroft?"

"I'm not a homosexual, if that's what you mean, Ricky." Stanley placed the huge vase of flowers on the coffee table and sat down in the lounge chair opposite him. "Now, what did you want to talk about?"

DeAngelo was intrigued. "If you ain't queer, why don't you have a woman?"

"I just haven't been that lucky, I guess," Stanley replied, a little too mournfully.

"Hey, luck ain't got nothing to do with it." DeAngelo leant forward and tapped the coffee table with his finger. "I'll find you a

nice Italian girl…yeah, a widow I know, very lonely. And
Bancroft," he said, and grinned, "in bed she'll do things you never
thought possible."

Stanley was about to protest when DeAngelo held up his
hand. "Now," he said firmly, "let's talk about our father, Roberto.
Yesterday he tried to kill himself, right?"

"Yes, Ricky," Stanley replied softly. "He tried to hang
himself."

"And last week, what that fat bitch manager said, did Poppa
faint and fall in the lake?"

"No. When I pulled him out, he had a piece of concrete tied
to his leg."

"Oh, shit," DeAngelo mumbled, then he buried his face in his
hands.

"Have you spoken with him, Ricky?" Stanley asked.

"No, the rope crushed the silly bugger's er…what's it
called?" he asked, touching his throat.

"His larynx?" Stanley suggested.

Yeah, that, but he writes us notes and, Jesus, he ain't happy
with you right now," Ricky said, and laughed loudly. "But hey,
you're family, right Bancroft? And we gotta look out for family.
Problem is, our father, he hates your guts, so I gotta look out for
you most of all." Ricky laughed again.

Stanley assumed it was a shared joke, so he laughed too.

"Hey," Ricky said, frowning at Stanley. "I wouldn't be
laughing if I was you. Do you know how many men my old man's
put away?"

Stanley moved uncomfortably in his chair. "Don't you think
you should keep him in hospital until he's feeling a little better?
Emotionally, I mean?"

DeAngelo was quiet for a moment. "Yeah, you're probably
right; a month or two inside would give us all a break, right
Bancroft?"

Without waiting for an answer, DeAngelo rose to his feet and made for the door. "This's a little somethin' extra for you." He nodded his head and scarface handed Stanley the metal briefcase.

"Hey, this is becomin' a habit, Bancroft. I dunno if I can afford you on my team," he said, and burst into laughter.

As the limousine sped off towards the security gates, a thought occurred to Stanley. How did DeAngelo get into the resort without a security card?

Stanley locked the front door, then eased himself into the chair just vacated by DeAngelo. He placed the briefcase on his lap and slipped the latches. When the lid flew open, Stanley stared in amazement—the briefcase was neatly packed with wads of money.

Chapter Ten

"I'm sorry my father isn't able to give you any time, Gerry, but he's expressed interest in your services, so he asked me to meet with you this morning."

Joshua Davenport leant back in his chair and extended the French cuffs of his business shirt beyond the sleeve of his custom tailored Italian suit. "Marketing and promotion is my field of expertise anyway. I handle that side of the business for all our company's major projects."

Gerry smiled as he took the seat being offered to him by the young man. Gerry was certainly not sorry. Davenport Junior was exactly the person he wanted to see. Despite his claims of importance within Joseph Davenport's empire, Gerry knew that he was a nonentity. While his father gave him an office on the company's twelfth floor, overlooking Cavill Avenue in Surfers Paradise, he had limited decision-making responsibilities. Joshua Davenport was more interested in attractive women, the Gold Coast's nightlife, and spending his father's fortune—mostly on attractive women.

Gerry flicked through his portfolio on Davenport's desk as he explained some of his recent projects. Even to the inexperienced young executive, Gerry's presentation was impressive.

"We work with the developer to produce a detailed prospectus, while offering an independent assessment of a particular project. Financiers and the various authorities like this approach. It reflects the observations and opinions of an outsider, and not the biased concepts of the developer."

Joshua Davenport nodded as he examined the material, not really listening to Gerry's preamble. What was of interest to him was the quality of Gerry's work, and how he could use the man to impress his father. The old man had rejected most of his proposals and scoffed at his efforts whenever he put forward his ideas and suggestions for a particular job. Now he saw an opportunity to use this man to help him gain his father's respect.

"Your work is excellent, Gerry," Davenport said, putting on his best business demeanour. "I think we may be able to do some business together." Davenport rubbed his chin and looked serious for a moment. "Tell me, Gerry, could you work with me secretly? Incognito, so to speak?"

Gerry looked surprised. "I guess so. Why do you ask?"

Davenport sat back in his chair and placed his hands behind his head. "Gerry, your portfolio indicates you are a competent businessman, able to work with your clients on confidential projects with discretion and integrity." He moved nervously in his chair. "Unfortunately, my father isn't like me, Gerry. He's not a trusting man. That's because we always have a number of projects in progress that are highly confidential, and if word were to leak out that Davenport Developments was involved, they could be placed in jeopardy. Do you understand what I'm saying, Gerry?"

Gerry nodded. He felt sorry for the young man as he tried to validate the role he played in his father's empire.

"If you did assist us with any of our projects, you'd be working directly for me. We'd meet outside this office, and I would personally pay you for your services." Davenport hesitated. "Now, on the subject of fees, what would you charge for something like this?" He removed a folder from Gerry's portfolio and held it up.

"That depends on travel. Doing work on the Gold Coast, for instance, would be more expensive than something near my base in Ballina and Byron Bay." Gerry paused for a moment. "If you have a project in my area, I'd be prepared to do it at cost so you can assess the quality of my work."

Gerry could see that Davenport was struggling to restrain his excitement. He was about to take the bait.

"Well, it so happens that there is a project we're looking at in your area, Gerry." Davenport rose to his feet and stood looking down on the Gold Coast traffic as it manoeuvred around the crowds of tourists who wandered aimlessly through the maze of clubs, coffee shops, and souvenir stores. "It's a major project, even for Davenport Developments, so I must ask you to treat what I'm about to say in the strictest confidence."

"Naturally," Gerry replied, trying not to appear over enthusiastic.

"Have you heard of Serenity Quays?" he asked.

"That's the retirement resort just north of Ballina?"

"That's the one. Our company is considering buying that resort," he said, as if the project were entirely his responsibility. "Would you be interested in helping me put together something on the proposal?"

Gerry could not believe his luck. He had come to Davenport Developments' Gold Coast office in the hope of obtaining a sliver of information about the rumoured sale. Now he was being offered a chance to work on the proposed acquisition. "I would like that very much, Joshua," he replied calmly.

"Good," he said. "Bear with me for a moment while I get the file from my father's office."

A few minutes later Davenport returned, holding a bulging file. He closed his office door and locked it. "You don't have any objections if we begin some preliminary discussions immediately, do you, Gerry?"

"I think that'd be an excellent idea," Gerry replied, hardly able to contain himself.

Davenport opened the file and turned its contents towards Gerry. Attached to the inside cover was a one-page document, titled *Preliminary Contract*. Joshua pushed the file a little closer and grinned boastfully as Gerry stared, in disbelief, at the amount, in bold print, on the document before him. Gerry moved uneasily in his chair. Joshua Davenport, in a childish display of business bravado, had allowed him to read the confidential details of the sale.

"Should I be seeing this?" Gerry asked.

Joshua looked embarrassed for a moment, then began to flick over the pages as he spoke about his father's plans to develop Serenity Quays. But Gerry was not fully focused on what Joshua was saying. It was difficult to take his mind off the details he had just seen on the contract.

Gerry was feeling guilty as he left Joshua Davenport's office and made his way to the lifts. He had allowed himself to be drawn into a deceptive relationship battle between a son and his father. Gerry's actions, if he were discovered, could be very damaging for his reputation—and his business.

Gerry was deep in thought when the lift doors opened and two men emerged. One he recognised immediately as Joe Davenport. The man with him looked familiar, and for a moment he wondered where he had seen him before. As they passed one another, the second man turned and nodded to Gerry. It was Dermot Bollinger.

As the lift door began to close, Gerry watched the two men walk towards the reception desk—he was sure that Bollinger hadn't recognised him.

A moment later, Dermot Bollinger turned towards the closed lift. The face of the person they had just passed seemed vaguely familiar to him.

* * *

Felicity Grimes was making her way towards the security gates. Walking for Felicity was a risk. In her car, the residents were unable to halt her progress, but on foot she was vulnerable. Residents waited on every corner, ready to assail her with complaints about insignificant problems that needed her immediate attention. But it was 8:30, and at that time of night, she felt relatively safe.

She had just paid a visit to Lily Hartmann in an effort to defuse the alarming situation with her neighbours, the Fisks. Felicity was concerned that if Lily took to Marty Fisk again, next time he could be seriously injured. Lily was inconsolable about her recently departed and much loved cocky, and she was determined to inflict as much punishment as she could on those responsible for her beloved bird's untimely demise.

As she passed Alison Arbuckle's house, something odd caught Felicity's attention. She stopped and listened to the music. It was not the country and western stuff she usually heard blaring from Alison's stereo—this was the lilting soprano voice of Sara Brightman, singing *Nessun Dorma*. It was one of Felicity's favourites.

Felicity noticed that Alison's car was still in the carport, and there was a reflection of light through the lounge room curtains. She was fascinated by the music, and, for a moment, considered paying Alison a visit to complement her on her choice of artist. She looked at her watch, but decided it was probably a little late for visiting. Felicity listened to the music for a moment longer, then continued on her way towards the exit gates.

* * *

From behind the curtains, Alison Arbuckle and Charles Badminton-Smyth watched Felicity disappear into the night. Alison smiled at Charles, who held her in a loving embrace. "For a moment there, I thought she was going to come and knock on the door," she said.

Charles kissed her on the neck. "Maybe we should turn the music down. We might be disturbing the neighbours," he whispered in her ear.

"Stuff the neighbours," Alison replied, and reached up and kissed him on the lips. "Now, tell me again how you're going to ravage my body when you get me into my bedroom."

* * *

Spencer J. Scraggs was a meticulous individual who prided himself on being a perfectionist. For many years, he worked for Dermot Bollinger as his spin-doctor, analysing Bollinger's ideas and putting them together on paper. Scraggs was an authority on everything, yet qualified in nothing. He failed his law degree exams despite eight years of study, and he had never qualified as a chartered accountant, although he was a highly competent bookkeeper. But Dermot Bollinger recognised Scraggs' talents, utilising his acquired skills to formulate his plans, and to help him present his projects to potential investors and government authorities. Scraggs could manipulate and distort the facts so expertly, that the projects put forward by Bollinger were able to withstand the closest scrutiny.

But that was five years ago. Now Bollinger was using him in a different capacity. Scraggs was living in Serenity Quays rent-free and, in return, he was responsible for manipulating Quinsy Naylor and the Tenants' Committee by offering his valued legal advice and business opinion. Spencer J. Scraggs not only convinced those he advised that he was a qualified solicitor and accountant, even he had come to believe the stories he peddled about his business qualifications.

"I've checked your figures and made some adjustments. You can spread all your losses through Long Haul Logistics," Scraggs said. "I estimate your costs to relocate each tenant and move their vacated houses to be a little under three thousand dollars. So, in reality, you'll make a profit of over two thousand dollars with each house that you move."

Long Haul Logistics Pty Ltd was a subsidiary transport business Bollinger used as a loss company to avoid income tax payments. "Are you sure Vertigo Properties Ltd won't need to record any of the transactions?" Bollinger asked cautiously.

"I've checked it thoroughly with an old mate of mine in the Tax Office —it's guaranteed," Scraggs replied.

"You've done a fine job, Spencer. Can you e-mail the information to me?"

"Will do. When do you intend to start moving us out?" Scraggs asked.

"Soon, Spencer, very soon." Bollinger hesitated. "We need you to select a block—are you available later in the week?"

This was the invitation Scraggs had been waiting for. "Friday would be suitable for me."

"Good. We're looking at several sites that may interest you near the main entrance. We'll place you as far away as possible from Naylor and his bunch of rabble," Bollinger said, and sniggered crudely. "After spending last weekend with him and that pisspot wife of his, there's no way I would inflict those people on any of my friends."

"I'd appreciate that, Dermot," Scraggs said, obviously relieved. "Is Naylor onside?" he asked.

"I believe he is, but the guy's a fool, so you and Arty Bullpit will need to guide him every step of the way. You know what I mean, Spencer?"

"Of course, Dermot," Scraggs replied. "Leave him to us."

Chapter Eleven

The police officer was fascinated by Agnes Hoskiss' story. Spiking the drinks of young women in clubs and bars was not uncommon, but a middle-aged woman in a retirement village—this was really quirky. The policeman was interviewing Agnes and her husband, Charlie, on the verandah of their home. He leant forward to ask Agnes another question when a man suddenly stood between them.

"I need to speak with you immediately," the man demanded in an aggressive tone.

"I really don't have time, sir. I'm here to investigate another matter." The policeman was annoyed by the angry man's intrusion into his interview.

"This is more important than that Sheila's bloody drink being spiked," Willy Hogan said through gritted teeth. "Something or someone has killed Jack Russell."

The police officer studied Hogan for a moment. "Show me," he said, getting to his feet and abandoning the interview with Agnes Hoskiss.

Charlie Hoskiss was annoyed. He was determined to find out who had tampered with his wife's drink at the dance on Saturday night, causing her to behave in a wanton and irresponsible manner. Charlie was disgusted with his wife's behaviour, particular the rumour that she got lost on the way home and passed out under a tree on the resort's driving range.

Charlie protested in vain as Willy Hogan and the policeman departed.

The policeman followed Willy as he hurried towards his property. He led the policeman to the rear of the house and down to the water's edge, where a small sandy beach formed at low tide.

"There!" Willy said, pointing to an area that had been recently disturbed. A small amount of blood was splattered across the sand and, to one side, a bloodied dog collar lay apparently bitten in half.

The policeman studied the area briefly then looked towards Hogan. "So who's this Russell person you say has been killed?"

"Person?" Willy replied aggressively. "It's not a person—it's my dog. He's a Jack Russell, you idiot."

The policeman instinctively placed his hand on his firearm and Willy took a step backwards. He realised immediately that calling this cop an idiot was not a smart move.

"Look," Willy said, trying to divert attention back to the crime scene, "something very big has come out of the water and attacked my Jack Russell. That's his collar lying in the sand."

The hand of police constable Foggerty remained poised, ready to take appropriate action, his gaze firmly fixed on the person who had just called him an idiot. Foggerty knew that he was not the smartest cop on the Force, that's why he was still a constable. But this arsehole just insulted him, and for a split second he seriously considered *taking him out*.

Bruce Foggerty, or Butch as his fellow officers called him, had the instincts of the wild animals he loved to hunt. He spent most holidays in the Territory, hunting buffalo and wild pigs. He had even blown away the odd crocodile in his time.

Now Foggerty's eyes turned slowly to where Willy was pointing, and he studied the area more closely. Something about it looked familiar, and it disturbed him. He moved closer, squatting down to inspect the sand and grassy bank. After a short time, Foggerty rose to his feet and paced out the area. He stood at the water's edge, then looked up to where the discarded collar lay. "Jesus bloody Christ," he muttered under his breath.

* * *

"Not another dead pet," Felicity Grimes said in dismay as she slumped back into her chair. The events of the past twenty-four hours had been too much for her, and she had already taken her second Valium for the day. "That dog of Hogan's was a pest," she added. "It was just a matter of time before someone did something rash."

"This looks a little more sinister," Scraggs replied. "Maybe you should let Dermot know the rumour that's circulating about the incident."

Felicity Grimes didn't trust Spencer J. Scraggs. He was a devious little man that seemed to have the ear of her boss, whom he apparently spoke to regularly. For that reason, Felicity was normally wary of what she said to the man.

"What rumour?" Felicity asked.

"The police think that the dog could have been taken by something in the canals."

"A shark? There's no shark in our canals," Felicity replied, waving her arm dismissively.

"Not a shark," Scraggs said, and smirked at her. "There's a suggestion that it could've been a large croc."

Felicity looked at Scraggs for a moment, then giggled. "Come on, Spencer, you can't be serious. Mr. Bollinger has more important things to do than listen to that sort of foolish nonsense."

Scraggs shrugged and rose to leave. "Please yourself, Felicity, but if you don't ring him about this, I will."

Felicity Grimes was delighted with Scraggs' response. Great, she thought, go ahead and make an ass of yourself you horrible little man.

"Ring him by all means, Spencer " Felicity said, then turned her attention to the neat pile of paperwork on her desk. "Maybe Dermot can arrange for a crocodile hunter to come down here and capture the thing for you."

* * *

The first photo shoot had gone without incident, although the strain was beginning to tell on young Hamish MacTaggit. He had requested that the summer models remain dressed until their individual sessions began. Despite his request, the three women had removed their clothes, then wandered about during the entire shoot in their gaping dressing gowns.

Benny and Maurice worked around the women, as if they were preparing floral arrangements at the Chelsea flower show. They teased hair, applied make-up, adjusted sets to conceal intimate body parts, and generally organised the entire summer display. MacTaggit was grateful for their assistance, since he was incapable of working in close proximity to the women. Even through the camera lens, his subjects appeared to him to be quite obscene.

Hamish MacTaggit's concept of the ultimate female form was the aesthetic beauty of a sixteen-year-old virgin leaping across a meadow in a flimsy shift. Consequently, the sight of his calendar girls, in all their corpulent nakedness, was almost unbearable.

Now, as he packed his gear at the end of the second day, Hamish was suffering acute depression. The thought of another three sessions surrounded by more of these obese and sagging female bodies weighed heavily on his mind. He was convinced it was more than he could possibly endure. Maybe, if he pleaded with his boss, he would find someone else to take over the project. Unlikely, though, he thought. As the junior member of the staff, *he* was given all the *crappy* work. But this job was different, just as his friend in the lab had predicted—this shoot would be a nightmare for the young man.

* * *

Felicity listened on the phone as the doctor outlined Olive Giltrap's condition. "My patient needs to get away from that place, Ms. Grimes, she's in a serious state of emotional stress." The doctor paused. "What sort of establishment are you running there, anyway?"

Felicity was unable to respond. She was stunned by Olive's experience, even more than her doctor was. Three days earlier, Olive had been walking Squiggle, her miniature poodle, near the clubhouse, when the dog became extremely excited. Squiggle jumped up on the glass doors of the gym and was barking frantically. There were no lights on in the gym when Olive peered into the dimly lit room to see what had caused Squiggle to act so shamefully. Exactly what Olive saw had been difficult for the poor woman to discuss, but Felicity was able to ascertain that Olive had observed Charles Badminton-Smyth and Alison Arbuckle enjoying an amorous encounter on the rowing machine.

"The two people involved have been barred from the gym— mainly because of the risk to our public liability insurance," Felicity said. "Apart from that, there's little more we can do, Doctor."

"First the trade in illicit sex drugs, and now this. I was planning to have my mother move into one of your resorts, but now I'm having second thoughts. Good day, Ms. Grimes," he said and slammed down the phone.

Felicity replaced the receiver and sat back in her chair with a concerned look on her face. Then she giggled and waved her hand at the telephone. "Well, stuff you, Doctor," she said. "Just because people are over sixty doesn't mean they can't have a bit of fun."

* * *

A gloomy atmosphere prevailed as the ladies mingled in the clubrooms, unable to believe the news they were hearing. The photographer had failed to arrive for the 'Autumn Girls' shoot, and the rumour was that he had left the country. There was great disappointment amongst the woman, particularly those ladies who were to be featured in the project. Now their plans for the naughty calendar were in disarray.

Sissy Witherspoon cleared her throat and called the meeting to order. "It appears our charming photographer phoned his young fiancée this morning and informed her their engagement was off," Sissy said.

"What a beast," Benny said to Maurice, causing some giggles from the women nearby.

"He was calling from Bali," Sissy continued, "where he'd just eloped with a young film processor from his work."

"Nothing but a monster," Maurice added, causing more titters from the ladies.

"When will he be back?" Trinity Du Pont asked.

Sissy looked dejected. "He's not coming back. Apparently he and the young man plan to open a photographic business together, providing holiday snaps for Aussie tourists."

Maurice turned to Benny "Young man?" he said excitedly. "Oh, how sweet, I just love elopements, don't you, duckie?" There was unrestrained laughter around the room.

Sissy spoke loudly, trying to make herself heard above the din. "Now, I've been asked to inform you that Moose…er, Michael Dart, has offered to take over the project."

A deathly silence fell over the room for a moment until Clarissa Van Hooganband, now known as Miss April, called out in a shrill voice, "No bloody way is that bastard seeing me naked!"

A loud chorus of *"here, here"* went up from the ladies.

"Well, it's decided then," Sissy said loudly. "We'll decline Mr. Dart's kind offer and wait until the company can provide a replacement photographer some time in the New Year."

Trinity Du Pont was devastated by the outcome. "But that'll mean our calendar will have to be deferred for twelve months."

"I'm afraid we have no choice, Trinity," Sissy replied. "Now, that leaves us without a major activity for this year. Does anyone have any new suggestions?"

"We could put on a musical for our Christmas party," Penny Applebee said. "There should be enough talent around here to create a good show for the residents."

"There's very little musical talent in this place," Buffy Bullpit said. "Besides, no one here would have a clue how to stage a musical."

"Penny could," Clarissa Van Hooganband said. "She was in show business for years—weren't you Penny?"

Penny nodded. "Yes I was, and I was also a drama teacher at a private girls' school in Sydney before I retired. My girls put on a very successful musical during the last year I was there, and it won an Eisteddfod. I think I still have the script and musical score at home."

Jo Jo Fisk scoffed loudly. "You want us to do a musical that some kids did—what's it called?"

"Grease," Penny replied.

Muriel Naylor made a derogatory sound with her lips and laughed loudly. "You want to put on Grease using the residents of Serenity Quays? You can't be bloody serious."

"Why not? There's some great songs in the show. We could make a few changes to the story line and turn it into a satire—based on our age group." Penny was thoughtful for a moment. "We could call it *Grease—The Past Generation*."

"I think it's a wonderful idea," Clarissa shrieked excitedly. "And Penny would be great in the Olivia Newton-John role."

Buffy Bullpit disliked Penny Applebee—she was a *Category 4,* and a potential troublemaker. But jealously was the real reason for Buffy's feelings towards Penny. Buffy Bullpit envied Penny because she was attractive, and had a nice figure. "You're too old for the role, Ms. Applebee, and besides, who could you get to play John Travolta's part?"

"I played a dancer in my theatre company's version of *Forty-Second Street* three years ago, Buffy, so I think I'm capable of doing the part, and there's bound to be someone who could…"

"My Maurice does a wonderful ensemble of Peter Alan songs," Benny interrupted. "If you could see him dancing on the piano and shaking his kanakas in his rendition of *I Go To Rio.*" Benny took a deep breath and placed his hand over his heart. "Oh, I feel quite faint just thinking about it."

"There we go," Penny said, pointing to Maurice. "We have our leading man."

Chapter Twelve

The explosion came at exactly 4 a.m., shattering the sleep of every tenant in the vicinity of the Fisks' home. As the dust began to clear, the police and fire services arrived and, for a time, there was general panic in the darkness. To everyone's relief, there were no injuries, but the Fisks' bedroom wardrobes and their contents, including twelve dozen bottles of Marty's prize winning home brew, were destroyed.

"You had twelve dozen bottles of home brew stored in your house—are you crazy?" the fire officer shouted above the noise of the fire engine motor.

"It needed to be stored in a dry, dark area—where else would you suggest?" Marty shouted back.

"Not in your house, that's for sure. Each bottle of home brew is a time bomb waiting to go off—and if one goes, they all go."

A police officer was picking through the rubble in their second bedroom when Marty returned inside. An overpowering smell of fermented hops, yeast, and stale beer hung in the air. Broken glass from shattered beer bottles littered the room, while the sliding doors of the wardrobe hung grotesquely at odd angles. The cracked mirror glass on the doors created distorted images of the policeman as he stepped between the broken bottles on the beer sodden carpet. "It's amazing that you two weren't cut by flying glass," the policeman muttered, as he continued his investigation of the scene.

Marty looked along the hall to the main bedroom where Jo Jo was trying to salvage some of her clothes, with little success. He knew he would need to keep his distance. Soon Jo Jo would cut loose—she had been very proud of her extensive wardrobe.

"You had some of your stock of home brew in your main bedroom, and the rest in this room, is that correct, Mr. Fisk?"

It was the same policeman who had visited their home a few days earlier to investigate the assault on Marty. "Yes," Marty replied, looking around with a dejected expression. "I had six dozen bottles in here, and about the same in our bedroom."

"Strange that both wardrobes should explode at the same time," the policeman said, more to himself than to Marty. "The two rooms are at opposite ends of the house."

"Maybe the vibration from one set off the other," Marty suggested.

"Well, there's no sign of deliberate sabotage, Mr. Fisk. It looks like you were the victim of some volatile home brew."

"Yeah, well, my house insurance will cover this, so I'll get them to come and do an assessment," Marty replied.

"Don't hold your breath, Mr. Fisk. I doubt if any insurance company would cover this lot. Didn't you know it's illegal to have this much home brew stored in your house?"

Marty looked towards the main bedroom where he could see Jo Jo examining her mother's mink stole. It resembled a large decomposed rat that had been pulled from a sewer pipe. "Bloody hell!" was all Marty could say.

"I'll leave you to clean up here, Mr. Fisk. There's nothing more I can do."

As the policeman left, Marty looked once more towards the bedroom, where Jo Jo was inspecting her newest evening gown, or what was left of it. He placed his head in his hands and moaned— this was not going to be a good day.

Marty decided he needed a smoke and retreated to his verandah. The first signs of daybreak were beginning to appear over the rooftops. As he removed a cigarette from the pack, he looked up and saw Lily Hartmann watching him from her kitchen window.

"Boom!" she said, emphasising the expression with a hand gesture, indicating an explosion. Then she threw back her head and laughed heartily as she moved away from the window.

Marty stared at Lily's window. I wonder if…but that idea seemed ridiculous. How *could* the silly old bitch get into my house and set off a bomb? He shook his head, as if to clear such a stupid idea from his mind. As the copper said, I'm the victim of some volatile home brew.

* * *

Gerry Curry stood at a large dining table in the Princess Suite of the Marriott Hotel in Surfers Paradise. On the other side of the table, Joshua Davenport studied the material Gerry had presented to him. As Gerry looked around the room, he guessed that Davenport Junior spent many hours in the suite entertaining his lady friends. There was a large bedroom off the main area with a king-size bed. The bed covers had been thrown back, and a pair of high-heel shoes lay on the floor nearby.

"This is excellent work, Gerry. How did you manage to get hold of all this material?" he asked, pointing to one of the large area maps spread out on the table.

Gerry shrugged. As a resident of Serenity Quays, he had access to all the resort's advertising and promotional literature. "What do you think of the golf course concept?" he asked, ignoring Davenport's question.

Davenport rubbed his chin. "My father's not into sporting facilities in his developments, Gerry, I don't know."

"Well, I feel this would give you the edge you're looking for. This area at the back of Serenity Quays is open public space. You can only access it through the resort, so the Council would gladly hand it over if it were going to be developed as a golf course." Gerry pointed to an area on the edge of the resort. "The golf course would enable you to develop an extra thirty building blocks along the eastern boundary of the course." Gerry tapped the planned layout with his finger. "You could promote all *this* area as an up-market residential golf course estate."

"But there's already a golf course on the site."

"Not really, Joshua. It's only one fairway—a short par-three golf hole. It's little more than a driving range."

"Isn't that enough?"

"No, Joshua. Believe me, I'm a golfer. It's like...like making love to a woman. You undo the first three buttons of her blouse, and that's as far as you go. It's very frustrating, actually."

Suddenly Joshua understood. "You're right, Gerry," he said, "that's not good."

"No, Joshua, it's not. Besides, the existing golf site has water views, so it's valuable land that should be used for housing."

Gerry watched Joshua taking notes frantically as he spoke, knowing that he was silently rehearsing what he would say to his father. "Gerry, I agree. That land *should* be used for housing, and I see now that the golf course idea really has merit. Daddy, er...Father would like the rationale behind that concept."

"Providing the resort with a nine-hole golf course will add significantly to the value of each block."

Davenport's excitement grew as he warmed to Gerry's proposal. "We could ask an extra one hundred thousand dollars per site," he said.

"You're also creating a broader market for yourself, Joshua," Gerry added. "A choice of canal sites for the boaties, and golf course sites for the golfers."

"This proposal could increase our capital gain from the project by as much as fifty percent." Joshua Davenport could hardly contain himself as he examined the material Gerry had laid out on the table. "What we need is a computerised image of the golf course proposal. Do you think you could do that for me…us, Gerry?"

Gerry studied the large aerial map he had provided. "We could create a broad spectrum photograph of all this area here, and superimpose an artist's impression of the course with the new resort and waterways in the background."

Joshua rubbed his hands together with delight. "That would help our presentation enormously." He looked over Gerry's shoulder. "Gerry, can you follow this up and get back to me as soon as possible?" He grinned and winked. "I'm afraid I'll have to end our meeting now. I have a pressing engagement."

Gerry turned and saw an attractive redhead standing in the bedroom doorway. She glanced at her watch, then glared at them both. It was obvious that he had interrupted her lunchtime entertainment. Gerry rose to leave. "I'll have this completed by the end of the week," he said, as he hurriedly packed and closed his briefcase.

"Great work, Gerry. The project is showing excellent potential," Joshua said with an air of authority, obviously intended to impress his *pressing engagement.*

* * *

"That's their final offer, Dermot—twenty-two and a half million, and vacant possession within six months. This is an interim agreement, but it's binding on both parties, subject to the usual clauses." Fiddlemore's casual manner gave the impression that he handled multi-million dollar deals every day.

"Could any of the *usual clauses* give Davenport the opportunity to terminate the contract before the settlement date?"

"Not really. There are the normal provisions, but nothing likely to terminate the sale. There's a reference to the gazetted land use clause, but that relates to problems that would make the land uninhabitable."

"What do they class as uninhabitable?" Bollinger asked.

Fiddlemore flicked through his paperwork. "Oh, the usual: earthquakes, landslides, extraordinary flooding—anything that would make the land unsuitable for residential development."

"We won't have any problems in that area; it's been zoned medium-density residential land for ten years. So, what else could cause the contract to fall over?"

"Your inability to provide vacant possession at settlement date in six months time."

"That's not going to be a problem either. We'll be gone in four months," Bollinger stated confidently.

Fiddlemore smiled smugly. "Well, let's sign the thing and get this bastard's money," he said.

* * *

Father O'Brien was preoccupied as he sat in the confessional. It was Saturday afternoon, and the ladies were doing the flower arrangements for mass. This was always a difficult time for the priest, and he was not fully attentive to the poor souls who shuffled endlessly into the tiny cubicles to confess their weekly sins. It seemed unfair that every Saturday, he, a celibate priest, was forced to endure the sordid details of the decadent behaviour of his parishioners. After all, he had feelings—and desires as well.

O'Brien absolved them when they expressed contrition for their misdeeds, knowing they would be back into their sinful ways after mass the following day.

He was deep in thought as he opened the sliding window and blessed the next sinner kneeling close to him. It was a familiar female voice that snapped him back into reality.

"Bless me, Father, for I have sinned…" O'Brien leant back in his chair and placed his hand over his face, as if to shield his identity from the confessor.

"I've had immoral thoughts, Father," the woman said softly.

The priest's heart began to pound rapidly, and a cold sweat broke out on his forehead.

"What were these thoughts, my child?" His tone was melodramatic—like a bad impersonation of Humphrey Bogart.

"I find myself yearning for a man of God, Father, and I'm a married woman."

O'Brien moved awkwardly in his chair. The seat was hard. It had been designed deliberately that way—not as a form of penance, but more to create sufficient discomfort to stop the priest falling asleep while hearing confessions.

"Can you not be strong, my love, er…my child, and turn away from these thoughts?" he asked in a trembling voice.

"No, Father. I think I'm in love with him—and I want him to have his way with me."

Father O'Brien was close to physical collapse. He was sweating profusely, his hands were trembling, and he was breathing erratically. His took a deep breath and leant towards the window.

"Before bedtime tonight, my child, say three Hail Marys and one Our Father, and…" he hesitated, "…and come to the presbytery after mass tomorrow so I can council you on this problem." He then slammed the sliding window of the confessional box shut.

O'Brien was not sure how long he sat in the chair, staring at the closed confessional window, but some time later the Monsignor came to investigate why there was a sudden build-up of people waiting to have their confessions heard.

Chapter Thirteen

George Mollitt removed the cockatiel from its cage, then stroked it gently before placing it on the back of a lounge chair. The bird preened its feathers for a moment, giving off a soft plaintive sound as it settled into its early morning routine. There was a ruffle of feathers as the cockatiel noisily took to the air, circled the lounge room, and fluttered down onto a small bowl of bird food on the kitchen table. A moment later, George joined the bird at the table. He, too, had a bowl, which contained cornflakes, fruit, and milk. The man and the parrot then began to eat their breakfast silently together, a practice they had shared since the death of George's wife several years earlier. Their relationship was cordial, though not close, but certainly better than the one between George and his late wife. The bird and the man accepted their association with one another for what it was—a palisade against the boredom and loneliness of advancing old age.

After breakfast, George would place the parrot on his perch that swung from the roof of his back verandah. After a time, the bird would fly off a short distance to the edge of the nearby lake. There, he would join George's neighbour, Alby Titmus, as the old man sat feeding the wildlife that visited his back yard each morning.

The bird's relationship with Alby was entirely different from the one he had with George. George and the bird had difficulty communicating with each other. Unlike George, Alby would sit and talk to the cockatiel for hours as it fossicked for tiny succulents that abounded in the thick grass and rushes beside the lake.

That morning, however, the parrot strayed too near to the water's edge. He had been warned by Alby to be careful of Boris, his large, green-eyed friend, who had a taste for poultry and other forms of bird life. Suddenly, there was a wild splash of water, and a moment later, the parrot was gone, except for a few pale grey feathers that gently floated away from the bank on the now calm surface of the lake.

* * *

Felicity Grimes waited patiently on the phone. She had rung the local police station to obtain information about their inquiries into the spiking of Agnes Hoskiss' drink at the Saturday Night Jive. Her subsequent behaviour was still the talk of Serenity Quays.

"Ms. Grimes, I'm constable Foggerty," the policeman said. "Were you aware I was at Serenity Quays yesterday morning, questioning one of your tenants?"

"Yes, I was and I'm anxious…"

"Were you also aware that I looked into another matter, concerning a missing dog?" the officer interrupted.

Felicity hesitated for a moment. "You're investigating what happened to Mr. Hogan's Jack Russell terrier?" she asked, unable to contain her amusement. "The police must have little else to do if they have time to go looking for missing animals."

"You may find this amusing, Ms. Grimes, but I'm of the belief that there's a dangerous predator loose in the waters around your resort."

Felicity laughed again, though now it was more a nervous giggle. "You're not going to give me that crocodile nonsense, are you? The nearest wild crocodile would be a thousand miles north of here."

"You may think it's nonsense, Ms. Grimes, but I don't. You see, I spend a lot of time in the Northern Territory, and I know croc tracks when I see them."

"Have you thought that this could be a prank?" All humour had gone from her voice now. "There are residents in Serenity Quays who get up to some stupid practical jokes."

"Some prank, Ms. Grimes. We found the dog's bloodied collar. It'd been ripped off the animal's neck."

"Maybe it was a shark." Felicity was now becoming concerned, particularly as she had sent Scraggs away, telling him to ring Dermot about the rumour.

"Sharks don't crawl out of the water to take their prey," he said.

"What do you plan to do?" Felicity asked nervously.

"We've called in an expert from Sea World. We expect him here in the next few days, so we'll come and see you when he arrives."

* * *

Felicity read the headline on the front page of the local newspaper again. She had received a number of phone calls from residents who were alarmed by the article. Now she was doing her best to convince everyone who called that the story was a hoax by the newspaper—like a joke on April Fools Day.

'Large Crocodile Menace In Serenity Quays Residential Resort.'

The article continued…'Just how a crocodile could get itself trapped in the resort's waterways and remain undetected is a mystery. But one local policeman is convinced that tracks found near one of the homes appear to be those of a huge, four-metre reptile.'

Felicity gasped as she read the next line.

'Unfortunately, the manager of Serenity Quays, Ms. Felicity Grimes, was not available for comment when this reporter called her today.'

Felicity slumped into her chair as she continued reading. 'One resident did, however, suggest that it was probably a certain overweight neighbour of his, who often went skinny dipping in the canal near his home. That particular person was once mistaken for a baby humpback whale, and, on another occasion, a pregnant dugong. There have been no attacks on humans by the reptilian intruder, although a dog has been reported missing. Would any reader who has seen a small brown and white dog in the company of a very large crocodile phone Constable Foggerty of the local constabulary or Ms. Felicity Grimes at Serenity Quays.'

Felicity threw the newspaper in the wastepaper basket and picked up the phone. There was a certain local newspaper reporter about to receive a verbal thrashing from a very angry woman.

* * *

The experts from Sea World arrived the following day towing a small research vessel fitted with enough sonar, underwater cameras, and recovery equipment to capture the Lock Ness Monster. Within minutes of the boat being launched, the biologist and his assistant were moving across the lake in a precise grid pattern—the search for the elusive reptilian giant had begun.

The reporter who wrote the newspaper article accompanied Felicity and Police Constable Foggerty as they made their way towards the canal at the rear of Willy Hogan's house. He was a little wary of Felicity Grimes after her tongue lashing the previous day, but he was anxious to get the latest word on the town's notorious monster. "We need a Yeti or Tasmanian Tiger to draw the tourists to our area," he said excitedly to Felicity.

Police Constable Foggerty stopped and turned on the young reporter. "Listen, mate, if you're going to treat this matter as a joke, you can piss off now. This's a serious investigation, and we don't need anymore of those smart arse comments you published in your newspaper yesterday."

The reporter, a pimply-faced young man, smiled nervously when he saw Foggerty's hand go to his sidearm as he spoke. He nodded his understanding and backed away, deciding to keep his opinions to himself in the future.

The search continued all day, as the vessel moved across the holding lake, then into the canals. Every inch of Serenity Quays' waterways would be searched, no matter how shallow the water. It was late afternoon when the search vessel, having canvassed the entire area, headed in towards the waiting police officer and the reporter. Felicity had lost interest in their activities, as had the small groups of people who had gathered at times throughout the day to make jocular comments and offer unwanted advice.

As the vessel swung in towards the two men waiting on the pontoon, the biologist appeared on the stern, giving the thumbs down. "Nothing, I'm afraid," he called to them.

As the boat turned away again, the men heard a loud, piercing siren emanating from inside the vessel. "Wait!" the biologist shouted, and dropped below. A few minutes later a large net was let out over the side. "I think we may have something," he called, as the vessel set off in a wide arc.

The news quickly spread around Serenity Quays, and as the vessel approached the small beach where the Jack Russell had been taken a few days earlier, a large crowd had gathered. The vessel swung its gantry towards the shore, and the winch began to drag its massive cargo from the turbulent waters, turned cloudy by the violent upheaval now taking place. There were gasps of disbelief as the giant monster was lifted by the straining gantry from the water, its slimy body glistening like some prehistoric creature from a primeval bog. There were gasps of horror as the chain holding the netted beast suddenly gave way under the strain and the net unravelled, sending the thing crashing to the ground.

Stunned, the crowd slowly edged forward and stared in amazement at the hideous sight before them. It was the rotting remains of some ancient river gum, covered with years of silt and slime.

Chapter Fourteen

Felicity Grimes sat slumped over her desk, her depression and despondency tempered by her second Valium of the day as she spoke to her contact at Head Office. "What's going on, Jean? Something big is happening, and I can't get any answers from the boss. He seems to be avoiding me."

Jean was the Head Office receptionist, and knew most of the gossip, confidential and otherwise, within the organisation. There was silence on the other end of the phone for a moment. "I'm not supposed to say anything, Felicity, but the rumour is that Serenity Quays is up for sale." Jean almost whispered her reply.

"I'm not in the mood for jokes, Jean. What's really going on?" Felicity asked.

"It's true, Felicity. Dermot and that creep Fiddlemore are down on the Gold Coast this morning, stitching up the deal."

There was a pause as Felicity recalled the recent sequence of inexplicable developments. Why had she not seen the warning signs? Serenity Quays was being sold off, right under her nose. "Does anyone else know?" Felicity asked.

"The whole office is buzzing with rumours about the sale— and I think some of your residents know as well."

"Who, for instance?"

"Some guy named Quinsy Naylor and his wife spent last weekend with the Bollingers at Bribie, and I know Dermot spoke to that doofus Scraggs about the sale. I heard part of their conversation."

Jean was warming to the conversation.

"You must be kidding me, Jean. There's no way Dermot would invite Naylor and his wife to his home. They're from another planet." Felicity reached for the bottle of Valium in her desk draw.

"He did, Felicity. There's a photo of them together in the social column of yesterday's local newspaper. I'll fax you the clipping."

Jean became concerned when there was no reply. She had never known her friend to be so despondent. "I'm sorry you had to hear it from me, Felicity," she said.

"Thanks, Jean," Felicity replied. "Can you call me when Dermot gets back to the office. This's *my* resort, and I want some straight answers from him." She popped a Valium in her mouth and swallowed hard. "He owes me, Jean, more than anyone else around this place."

"You'll probably see him before we do, Felicity. I think he was heading your way after he left the Gold Coast."

Felicity hung up the phone and sat staring out the window. "The bastard may regret bypassing me with whatever he plans to do with Serenity Quays," she mumbled.

* * *

"I need to turn some of the water flow from this area back into the watercourse that feeds our main canal system," Bollinger said, indicating the direction with a sweep of his arm. "Is that possible?"

The two men had met on a dirt road used by the Rural Bush Fire Service in the hills above Serenity Quays.

The engineer stepped forward and visually surveyed the slope of the land. The course of two creeks had been redirected to take water run-off from the surrounding hills into a tidal river and out to sea through a narrow bay. Bollinger had engaged Dwayne Gannet on numerous projects in the past. He usually called on him to help organise jobs that required the utmost discretion, as they often bypassed government and environmental regulations and land development requirements.

Gannet was happy to plan and organise this work, providing the money was right and Bollinger took full responsibility for anything that was done illegally. But this proposal was plainly stupid, and that made Gannet curious. What sort of devious scheme, he asked himself, was the cunning old bastard up to this time?

"Turning the water run-off back down this hillside wouldn't be a problem, Dermot. It's the natural watercourse." He looked back at Bollinger. "But why would you do that? If there's a high tide during heavy rain, the river could overflow into the canals and flood the homes in your resort."

Bollinger smiled to himself. That was precisely the situation he wanted to create. "Could the work be done without attracting attention?"

"Depends how much water you want to go down there," Gannet replied.

Bollinger was thoughtful for awhile. "Let's assume we wanted to direct enough water into the canals to create some low-level flooding in the resort after, say, a few inches of rain."

Gannet turned and scampered up the hill a short distance to where the two creeks came close together. He squatted down and looked through an instrument he carried on a cord around his neck. Both creeks had been deepened, then redirected away from the resort when it was being built ten years earlier. He looked down the steep hillside to a small artificial lake near the entrance of the resort. He shook his head and returned to where Bollinger was waiting for him.

"Well?" Bollinger asked in an abrupt tone.

Gannet looked concerned. "You could redirect the water flow from the larger creek," he said, pointing up the hill. "But Jesus, Dermot. In really heavy rain, there's no saying what could happen. If your lake down there floods when the river is at high tide, there'll be nowhere for the water to go except into the canals. The whole resort could go under."

"What's the chance of that happening in the next few months?" Bollinger asked.

Garnet shrugged. "Who knows? It's been pretty dry lately, but they're saying El Nino is finished and we may be in for a long wet period." Gannet looked confused. "Why only a few months?" he asked.

Bollinger looked down towards the resort in the distance. He knew, with some reluctance, that he would have to confide in Gannet. "I want to scare the residents a bit. I want to move everyone out and close Serenity Quays. If we can create some minor flooding on the resort, it may make our job of persuading the tenants to move a little easier."

Gannet looked at Bollinger and grinned. The old prick has had an offer to buy his residential park—that's why he wants to get rid of everyone. Well, I'm going to get a piece of *this* action, he thought.

"The odds of serious flooding in that short period of time is not very likely, but it's risky. If I'm caught, I could lose my New South Wales license. I'd need ten grand to complete the work on such short notice."

"How long?" Bollinger asked.

"Two days, maybe three, and I could start tomorrow."

"Ten grand for two or three days work? That's highway robbery."

"What we're doing could be regarded as a criminal offence, Dermot." He smiled and slapped him on the shoulder. "But think of the profits you'll be making from the sale of Serenity Quays. It makes my costs seem insignificant."

Bollinger was thoughtful for a moment. Gannet was a brilliant engineer, but he was also an opportunist and a person who could not be trusted. From their very first project together,

Bollinger had been cautious. He had made sure there was incriminating evidence of Gannet's involvement in any dodgy activities they had undertaken together. He had been particularly careful with the extensions to Hideaway Cove, where he had photographed Gannet working with his crew and equipment clearing the land. Bollinger had gathered sufficient evidence against Gannet to guard himself against any future problems with the man.

Bollinger smiled. "We're a long way from finalising anything on Serenity Quays, Dwayne, so I'm the one taking all the risks. You don't begrudge me making a little profit on the transaction if it comes off, do you?"

Gannet shrugged. "It's your neck, Dermot. What you do is your business. Do you want me to go ahead?"

"Yes," Bollinger said, "but we need to cover ourselves in case anyone asks what you're doing up here. I want a written quote before you start. It'll be for upgrading work you're carrying out on the creeks that divert water run-off away from the resort. Can you get your equipment up this access road?"

"Leave it to me, Dermot." Gannet grinned. "And stop worrying. No one will know what we're doing."

* * *

Felicity sat tight-lipped, glaring fiercely at Dermot Bollinger as he endeavoured to explain his reasons for selling Serenity Quays. The global warming story was not working—she was too smart for that yarn. He always knew it would be difficult explaining his actions to Felicity, but her anger surprised him.

"The reason I didn't tell you before this, Felicity, was because the negotiations were highly confidential."

"Scraggs knew. So did Naylor and half the office—why am I just finding out today? And what happens to me once this place closes?"

"There's a management opportunity for you at our Forest Lodge resort," Bollinger said cautiously.

"That's in Tasmania—I'm not going to Tasmania." She glared at Bollinger. "What about Hideaway Cove?"

"We already have a resident manager at Hideaway Cove."

"Well, you don't need me here anymore, do you? I'll want two days to pack my things and arrange for a removalist." Felicity began clearing her desk—she was close to tears.

There was a look of astonishment on Bollinger's face. "You're resigning now?" he asked.

"Yes, Dermot, I've resigned, as of now."

"What will you do, where will you go?" he asked.

"Not to bloody Tasmania, that's for sure." She looked at Bollinger, and there was anger in her eyes. "I have a friend who wants me to move in with him, and I can get work locally."

"You can't walk out on me, Felicity, not after all I've done for you."

"What *you've* done for me?" Felicity managed to laugh. "Dermot, I've worked my butt off keeping this place running efficiently for eight bloody years, and now you want to dump me in Tasmania."

Bollinger was alarmed—he needed Felicity to supervise the move. This was going to be a major task, and there was no one else in his organisation capable of handling the residents of Serenity Quays. "Well, what do you want me to do?" he asked, realising that Felicity had the upper hand.

Felicity stopped clearing her desk. "Employ me as resident manager for stage two of Hideaway Cove," she said.

Bollinger was thoughtful for a moment. There were no plans for a second resident manager at Hideaway Cove, but he was trapped. "Okay," he said, "you're hired."

"With a five year contract, a house that's not attached to an office, and a ten percent wage increase," Felicity added.

"Jesus, Felicity, you're taking advantage."

"Yes, Dermot, for the first time, I am."

Chapter Fifteen

Penny Applebee joined the three men sitting on Gerry Curry's back verandah. "My daughter e-mailed me this article from her local newspaper. She thought we might be interested." Penny handed the newspaper article to Tony Bloom. "Seems our friend Quinsy Naylor has friends in high places."

Gerry was briefing Tony and the Major about his meeting earlier in the week with Davenport Developments when Penny Applebee arrived with her piece of news.

Tony studied the photograph, then handed the clipping to Gerry. "Why is the chairman of our Tenants' Committee being entertained at the home of Dermot Bollinger, I wonder?"

"And why haven't the residents been told what transpired during this intimate get-together?" Gerry added, as he read the caption under the photograph.

"It could be something to do with Bollinger offering to move Naylor to his resort on the Tweed Coast," Penny said.

"To Hideaway Cove, who told you that?" Tony asked.

"Willy Hogan just told me," Penny replied. "It's supposed to be a secret, but Naylor got drunk at the sports club last night and started bragging. He claims we're all going to be given the opportunity to move there."

Tony turned to Gerry. "So that's how Bollinger's going to implement his devious little scheme. The bastard's going to try and move us all to Hideaway Cove."

"What scheme?" Penny asked.

"Bollinger's negotiating the sale of Serenity Quays, but the buyer's insisting on vacant possession. He has to remove all the houses, the clubhouse, the sports club—everything. Serenity Quays is going to become an up-market residential canal estate," Gerry replied.

"This's more serious than we thought," the Major said. "I think we should have a meeting of our action committee. I'm giving Badminton-Smyth and Sissy Witherspoon a call and see if they can get over here right away."

* * *

"Ooh, bloody hell," Benjad Rumanackrin of the Weather Bureau mumbled, as he studied the movement of a deep low forming off the New South Wales coast. "Where did you come from, you nasty little bugger?"

"What have you got for us, Benjy?" his boss asked, leaning over the monitor. Benjy was one of the Bureau's top men, and could smell a rain depression before it appeared on the radar.

"A rain depression forming off the North Coast, Boss—a big one," Benjy replied with an air of excitement. "Moving west-southwest at twenty knots. Should cross the coast near Byron Bay late tonight or early tomorrow."

* * *

Exactly as Benjy predicted, a severe storm with thunder, lightning, and heavy rain crossed the coast at around 12:30 a.m. that night, between Byron Bay and Ballina. Almost a hundred millimetres of rain fell in three hours, causing local flooding in a number of areas.

One of those areas was Serenity Quays, where water covered the whole estate to a depth of ten centimetres. Because the ground was relatively dry, there was good run-off, and no water entered any of the homes. By around midday, most of the water was gone from the resort.

* * *

"Well, that's it for me," Willy Hogan proclaimed loudly. "I'm outer here. Next time we mightn't be so lucky. I'm taking Bollinger up on his offer and movin' to Hideaway Cove as soon as I can."

It was late afternoon, and the men sat around in the sports club discussing the flash flood that had inundated the resort the previous day. All sports activities had been abandoned, the members preferring, instead, to talk about the storm while doing some serious drinking.

"What I want to know is, where did all that water come from?" Gill Trotter looked out through the sports club windows and was thoughtful for a moment. "It's rained like that before and the place hasn't flooded."

"I told you, Gill, Serenity Quays is three metres below sea level. As the wet weather increases with global warming, these low-level areas will go under." Quinsy had been practicing his prepared speech, and now it was almost word perfect.

"Global warming, my arse. We're in the middle of a drought," Clarry Humphries mumbled, as he poured his sixth glass of home brew.

"I agree with Quinsy," Arty Bullpit declared. "Another storm like last night, and we could have water right through our homes. The Hideaway Cove deal looks pretty good to us."

"We can't afford the six grand Bollinger wants us to pay for the move to Hideaway Cove," Marty Fisk said, looking despondent. "My bloody insurance company knocked back our claim for the repairs after my home brew exploded, so now I'm broke."

"You can add the payment to your weekly rent and pay it off over five years," Quinsy replied.

Bert Pugh grunted with indignation. "I don't see why we should have to pay anything," he said, opening a can of beer. "You can bet your balls Bollinger will make a fortune from the sale. Why isn't *he* carrying the cost to move us outa here?"

"Because we're going into an up-market resort," Arty Bullpit responded. "We're all gonna be better off financially."

"Yeah, particularly that bastard, Bollinger," Marty Fisk replied.

"Get off it, Marty," Quinsy Naylor said. "Dermot Bollinger's a good bloke."

"Just what's your connection with Bollinger, Naylor?" Hank Van Hooganband asked. "You're always defending the bastard, and you run around kissing his arse whenever he comes to Serenity Quays."

"What exactly do you mean by that?" Quinsy asked, rising unsteadily to his feet.

"Come on, you two, we're here to have a few beers, not a punch up." It was Bullpit who intervened.

"I'd still like to know why so much water came into the resort," Gill Trotter repeated. "The runoff from that amount of rain should have been able to get away."

* * *

"What's Felicity Grimes saying?" Gerry asked. "She must have some opinion why there was so much water around the resort." The action group had gathered on the Major's verandah to discuss the effects of the previous night's storm.

"High tide and a lot of rain, she claims," Tony replied.

"We've had heavier rain than that before," the Major said. "Something must have happened to cause that much water to inundate the resort."

"Like what?" Sue asked. "Are you suggesting some sort of conspiracy, Major?"

"Maybe. It just seems odd that it's happened now—with the move on, I mean," the Major responded.

"Grimes was wrong about one thing. The tides had nothing to do with it," Tony said. "It wasn't high tide until two hours after the rain had cleared."

"Well, it's got everyone panicking now. Some of the residents can't get out quickly enough," Sue commented.

"In my opinion, there's more to this than meets the eye," the Major said.

Gerry Curry listened to the others express their views as to what caused the brief flooding in the resort. He, too, had concerns about the timing of the incident, and why the resort would flood after a brief storm. And there was his business relationship with Joshua Davenport. He enjoyed working with the young man, and he felt some obligation to advise him of what had occurred. He would ring Joshua, he decided, and suggest his father check the contract in relation to vendor disclosure and the likelihood of flooding in Serenity Quays.

* * *

Dermot Bollinger felt uneasy about his visitor—they usually did their business on site, not in his office. This was an emergency, however, and he had insisted that Dwayne Gannet get himself up to his Maroochydore headquarters for a crisis meeting without delay. Twenty-four hours later, Gannet sat in Bollinger's office, annoyed at being dragged away from the job he was working on in Brisbane.

"What's so important that you needed me here on such short notice?" Gannet asked.

"We had some minor flooding at Serenity Quays two days ago," Bollinger replied.

Gannet laughed. "Well, I did warn you, Dermot."

Bollinger smiled and lounged back in his leather office chair. "Yes, Dwayne, we achieved what we wanted to do, so now I want you to turn the water runoff back the way it was. I don't want anyone snooping around up there to see what caused the flooding the other night."

"I can't afford to be going backwards and forwards to New South Wales, Dermot. I've got my business in Brisbane to run."

Bollinger glared at the young man. "I'm not asking you, Dwayne, I'm telling you. I want the creek wall repaired."

"Well, it's going to cost you. Restoring the wall of that creek was not included in my original quote," Gannet replied.

"Bullshit. You knew this'd be necessary once we achieved our objective. Ten grand was a rip-off to begin with." Bollinger pointed a finger at Gannet. "The restoration work should have been included in your original price—and I want the job done immediately."

Gannet sat glaring back at Bollinger across the desk. He was unsure how hard to press the issue—he hadn't been paid for doing the initial work. But Dwayne Gannet was an aggressive young man, and he was determined that Bollinger would not get the better of him.

"You're a greedy bastard," Gannet said, his jaw fixed in anger. "You're going to make a fortune from the sale of Serenity Quays, and I'm helping you do it. I want to be paid for the work I've already done, Dermot, and another five grand to restore the creek back to the way it was."

Bollinger got to his feet and strolled over to his office window, standing with his back to Gannet. "Dwayne, you and I have worked together on a number of projects over the years." He turned back towards the young man, and there was a defiant look on his face. "I'm a very careful businessman, Dwayne. I systematically record every detail of the projects I undertake, in particular those…slightly irregular projects that involve you. In fact, I've gone out of my way to record the work you've done for me."

Bollinger returned to his desk and opened a manila folder, labelled *Gannet Engineering Services Pty Ltd.* He removed a number of photographs, then laid them out in front of Gannet, like a dealer in a game of poker.

Gannet studied the photographs for a minute, then laughed, waving his arms in dismissal. "You'll implicate yourself if you show these to the authorities."

"Maybe, Dwayne, but this is *you* driving the machinery that's dumping building waste in a native wetland, and this is *you* in the bobcat, knocking down pristine native forest." Bollinger picked up one of the photographs and studied it closely. "And that's *you* driving the truck with your company name on it. It's loaded with protected forest timbers that your men can be seen felling in the background. No, Dwayne, you're the one they'll throw the book at if the authorities get hold of these photos." Bollinger sat down at his desk. "My barristers will argue that you went beyond my instructions and took it on yourself to carry out this wanton environmental vandalism." Bollinger hesitated. "Do *you* have a good barrister, Dwayne?"

Gannet sat staring at the photographs, but said nothing.

"You should take those with you, Dwayne, just in case you get any silly ideas. I've several sets of prints if I need them."

Gannet looked up at Bollinger. "You really are an arse hole, Dermot," he said, scowling angrily at the man.

"I'm sorry you have that attitude, Dwayne, because now we're going to renegotiate your original quote. I think a figure of three thousand dollars is more realistic," he said, tapping one of the photographs. "Of course, that fee will include restoring the water runoff back to its original course—right, Dwayne?"

Gannet gritted his teeth. "Right," he replied.

"Now, how about we call an end to this little get-together. We both have work to do." Bollinger turned to a document on his desk and began reading it.

When Gannet reached the office door, he turned to Bollinger. "Once this job is finished, you can find someone else to do your dirty work," he said, his face reddened with anger.

"Oh no, Dwayne," Bollinger replied. He selected one of the photographs and held it up to him. "You and I have a life-long contract now."

Gannet stormed from the office and slammed the door behind him.

* * *

"That's very good, Maurice," Penny said, as she played the last few bars of, *You're The One That I Want.* "Where did you learn to dance like that?"

Maurice did a graceful pirouette, then glided over to where Penny Applebee, Benny, and Clarissa Van Hooganband were standing by the piano.

"I was a regular dancer on the old *Melbourne Tonight Show,* back in the early seventies."

"Doesn't he look positively divine in leather?" Benny remarked, as he gazed at his partner with admiration.

Only Penny and Maurice had arrived for the first rehearsal. The other residents who were to participate in *Grease—The Past Generation,* had failed to appear. Clarissa had volunteered to be stage manager, while Benny would create the stage scenery and lighting. Everyone else, it seemed, were too busy packing for the move to Hideaway Cove.

"I'm afraid we'll have to abandon our plans for the show," Penny said, running her fingers dejectedly along the piano keys. "No one has time for rehearsal, with the move to Hideaway Cove before Christmas." Penny sighed deeply. "I was looking forward to our stage show; it was going to give me an interest for the next few months." Penny closed the piano and looked around the room. "I'm becoming awfully bored with this place."

"Why don't you take up lawn bowls with me," Clarissa suggested. "Its fun, and it keeps you active."

"Bowls?" Penny exclaimed loudly. "I'm not ready for bowls just yet, Clarissa."

"School kids play bowls now, Penny. It's becoming a young persons' game. I've got a *roll up* this afternoon. Why don't you come?" Clarissa asked.

"What's a roll up?"

"A training session, where you learn how to bowl. I've a spare set you can use."

"You won't get me into one of those awful white outfits bowlers wear," Penny said, with a determined look on her face.

"At my club the women bowlers wear a nice colourful uniform," Clarissa replied. "Besides, there's no dress regulations for beginners. You can wear what you like."

"You'd better not wear those black tights you have on now, sweetie," Maurice said, studying Penny's backside with one hand cupped under his chin. "You might give those old farts a heart seizure when you bend down to bowl."

Chapter Sixteen

"Team five," a loud voice called from the doorway to the greens. "I need Applebee and...oh, bugger." There was a momentary pause. "And Joycie Livermore," the voice called.

"What rotten luck," Clarissa said. "Mabel Munzie—the dragon lady herself."

Penny looked in the direction Clarissa was pointing and saw a woman leaning on a walking stick. Mabel Munzie appeared to be in her seventies, and crippled with arthritis.

"Fancy getting her as skip," Clarissa said, shaking her head. "And in your first match."

Penny sensed a feeling of uneasiness—doubtful that she was ready for her first competition match. Several practice sessions earlier in the week had indicated that she was a little *heavy handed* with the bowl.

"You'll have to speak loudly or she won't hear you," Clarissa warned, as they made their way towards the woman waiting impatiently by the door.

"What's your first name again?" the woman asked, after being introduced by Clarissa.

"Penny," she replied.

"Okay, Polly, I'm your skip. You'll be our lead, and spaghetti brains over there can be our third."

Penny felt awkward. She had little idea of the rules, or what was required of the lead player. "I've never played before," Penny said nervously.

Mabel glared at her. "We don't have a number four—haven't you played this game before?"

Penny sighed. "I just said..."

"Okay, then," Mabel interrupted. "If you want to play third—behind that basket case," she said, pointing to Joycie. "Go ahead, but don't say I didn't warn you, Polly."

"My name's Penny," she said loudly, but Mabel didn't appear to hear her.

Clarissa whispered some parting words of encouragement to Penny as she and Mabel made their way towards an elderly woman sitting at one end of the green, polishing her bowl.

"This is Polly, Joycie," Mabel said. "She's on our team today."

"The name's Penny, actually," Penny said, extending her hand to the old woman.

"G'day," the woman replied, without looking up from her polishing.

Penny watched as Mabel got the match under way. The woman, restricted by her arthritis, leant heavily on her walking stick as she bent down and bowled a small white ball called *the jack* to the other end of their rink. The ball rolled along the green like a slow-motion replay before it came to rest at the other end.

Penny heard a cry and turned to see Mabel still kneeling on the mat, a distressed look on her face. "Help me," she called, "I can't get up."

Penny rushed to Mabel's aid, but Joycie remained seated, chortling loudly at her playing partner's discomfort.

"Bloody bitch," Mabel muttered, as Penny helped her to her feet. Mabel glared angrily at Joycie as she adjusted her clothing, then made her way slowly to the other end of the rink.

Their three opponents, who were from a neighbouring club, watched the altercation between the two women with amusement. When they had played their shot, Joycie stepped up to the mat.

"Put your bowl on this side of the jack, Joycie," Mabel called to her.

Joycie mumbled something inaudible, then guided her bowl gracefully along the green, where it came to a halt a short distance from the jack—on the opposite side to where Mabel had indicated. Penny watched, fascinated, as the two women stood at opposite ends of the green, hands on hips, glaring at one another.

When Penny prepared to have her turn, Mabel called to her. "Try and place it here, Polly," she shouted.

"Who the hell is Polly?" Joycie asked, as Penny was about to bowl.

Penny stifled a laugh as the bowl left her hand and she watched it wobble erratically towards the other end. Surprisingly, it finished up only a short distance from where Mabel had indicated.

On Joycie's next turn, Mabel stood over the jack. "Try and get it right this time, Joycie. Put your next bowl here," she said, prodding the air with her stick.

"In your dreams, shit face," Joycie said, loud enough for those around her to hear. She bent down and sent her bowl firmly along the green, striking the jack a perfect blow, and hurling it into the gutter at the end of the green. She turned to Penny and winked.

Penny was feeling nervous as she picked up the bowl for her next shot. "Put your bowl on this side, Polly—about here," Mabel called loudly. Several players on the adjoining rinks glared and shook their heads. It was obvious to Penny that her skip's loud, penetrating voice was becoming an irritation for the other players.

As Penny bent down to play her shot, she was totally focused on the small white ball at the other end of their rink. "Your bias is wrong, love," a voice behind Penny said quietly, distracting her concentration completely.

"What?" Penny said, standing and facing Joycie, who was vigorously polishing her remaining bowl.

"Thunder thighs wants you to put your bowl on the right, so you'll need to reverse the bias."

123

"Get on with it, ladies," Mabel shouted from the other end. "This isn't a garden tea party."

Penny looked at her bowl. That's not what she was told at her training sessions. She looked back at Joycie, who was still polishing furiously, and the old woman smiled at her.

"You remind me of my daughter," Joycie said, cocking her head to one side. "You're not my daughter are you, love?" she asked.

Penny was about to reply, then shrugged. Reverse the bias, she said to herself, and bent down and played her shot. Penny watched her bowl as it gathered speed. It was a perfect shot, she thought, as the bowl began its wide sweeping arc, exactly as Joycie indicated it would.

A loud, melancholy groan from Mabel Munzie startled Penny at the same time as her bowl made a sudden, erratic turn to the right. Everyone watched in dismay as Penny's bowl crossed their rink, then slammed into the adjoining teams' cluster of bowls, scattering them in all directions—most of them into the gutter.

There was stunned silence around the greens, except for the muffled giggle of Joycie Livermore, as she continued polishing her bowl.

"That's it," Mabel shouted to the opposing skip. "We're forfeiting the game," she said, as she collected her bowls and stormed off the green.

"So tell me, Jenny," Joycie asked, as she and Penny gathered up their gear. "How did you enjoy your first game of lawn bowls?"

"Is it always like this?" Penny asked, watching the fuming Mabel Munzie hobble into the clubrooms.

"No, fortunately," Joycie replied, and chuckled wickedly. "Some days it can be quite interesting."

* * *

Monsignor Montague Hopgood cleared his throat loudly as he tried to gain the attention of the women seated around him. The Monsignor was chairing the ladies auxiliary meeting in the absence of Father O'Brien.

Damned new age clergy, he said to himself. They think they can go running off whenever it suits them.

Monty, as he was called amongst his fellow clerics, felt uncomfortable when he was around the ladies of the auxiliary. He disliked most women, and this lot of noisy females was no exception. O'Brien had no trouble handling them, he recalled. Probably because of his rugged good looks and charming personality. He looked about him and shook his head—bunch of horny old bags, he thought to himself.

Monty was now on his own, deserted by his fellow priest, the man he relied on to take most of the workload in their large parish. O'Brien had renounced his ministry, packed his bags, and left for North Queensland, virtually overnight. Now Monty had the job of organising everything—and with little likelihood of a replacement in the immediate future. The priesthood used to be a privileged vocation, but not anymore.

"Ladies, may I have your attention? We have a very serious matter to discuss." His comment appeared to work, and the room suddenly fell silent. "Some of you may be aware that Father O'Brien has decided to take a sabbatical, and will be away for some time." What a stupid remark, he said to himself. This lot of blabbermouths probably knew about O'Brien leaving the Church before he did.

"We heard that he'd given up the priesthood," Hilary Ottoman remarked.

The priest looked at the person who had just spoken and decided that of all the women in the auxiliary, he liked her least of all. She was from that Serenity Quays place, where the Hoskiss woman lived—the one responsible for all the trouble.

"Father O'Brien has made no firm decisions about his future, Mrs. Ottoman. In the meantime, we still have work to do, so I'm taking responsibility…"

"We also heard that Agnes Hoskiss has resigned from the auxiliary," Hilary interrupted, "and from her marital responsibilities as well. Is that correct, Monsignor?" she asked.

The Monsignor took a deep breath—the woman was really testing his patience. They all knew that Agnes had walked out on her husband, and probably wouldn't be returning.

"Yes, sadly. I have spoken at length with Charlie Hoskiss, and he informs me that he and Agnes have separated, and she has moved to Sydney to live with her sister." The Monsignor bowed his head slightly. "Our prayers go out to Charlie and Agnes in the hope they will soon be reunited in the bounds of holy matrimony."

"Is Father O'Brien also going back to Sydney for his, er…his sabbatical, Father?" There was a sarcastic tone in Hilary's question.

There was a low murmur in the room—and someone sniggered. The Monsignor looked at the woman with contempt. For a moment, he had a sickening urge to jump to his feet and strike her down. He clenched his fist momentarily and waited for his anger to subside. As he did so, he considered the consequence of a violent confrontation with the woman. He smiled when he imagined the headlines on the front page of the Catholic Weekly. *Priest charged with assaulting a member of his Ladies Auxiliary.*

When the Monsignor spoke, he had regained his composure. "No, Mrs. Ottoman, Father O'Brien will be going in the other direction. Brendan has purchased an old fishing trawler from a friend in Cairns. For the next few months, he'll be spending his time restoring the boat, then doing some recreational fishing around the Whitsundays." He glared at Hilary Ottoman. "Now, is there anyone else you would like to inquire about, or are we free to get on with our meeting?"

* * *

Dizzy Abood was twenty-one and drove a bus. Not a big one like his father drove—his was a mini-bus, licensed to carry a maximum of sixteen passengers. Dizzy's father didn't think his son was smart enough to drive the big bus, so Dizzy was relegated to doing the small, casual jobs, usually taking kids to picnics and parties, or old people to bingo and bowls.

Dizzy lived with his parents, a younger sister, and his grandmother in the Northern Rivers town of Lismore, where they ran their small passenger bus business. Dizzy had few friends, and spent most of his time on the Internet, where he had become fascinated with the activities of al-Qaeda, and their jihad against Westerners—particularly Christians and Jews.

Dizzy's problem was that he was a Christian himself, he was a fan of the Sydney Bulldogs football team, and, being a second generation Australian, was regarded as a Westerner. And this was Dizzy's dilemma. His ambitions to join the terrorist movement were undermined because he had difficulty convincing anyone that his cause was either sincere or legitimate.

When he outlined his plans to his parents over dinner one night, his father laughed so much he was unable to finish his meal. Unlike her husband, Dizzy's mother saw nothing funny in her son's aspirations, and rushed from the table, weeping loudly. His sister giggled, and called him a dork, while his grandmother, a crusty old matriarch from the back streets of Beirut, shook her head sadly, then slapped him, hard, across the face. From that point on, Dizzy decided not to mention his ambitions to his family again. But Dizzy was a determined young man—and he had a plan.

That evening, Dizzy's father was giving him instructions about the following day's work. He was to pick up sixteen senior bowlers from a retirement resort called Serenity Quays and take them to Hideaway Cove Resort at Tweed Heads. He was to remain with the group, then bring them back later in the day.

"What'll I do all day?" he asked his father. "Why can't I come home after I drop them off, then go back for them in the afternoon?"

"Because of the petrol costs, you stupid boy," his father replied in an arrogant tone. "If you don't want to watch them playing bowls, sit in the bus and read a book." He glared at his son. "You do know how to read, don't you, Dizzy?"

"I don't want to spend the whole day with a bunch of old fogies," he replied stubbornly.

Dizzy rebounded in his chair as his grandmother leapt to her feet and slapped him firmly across the face.

As Dizzy lay in bed that evening, he decided he would bring his plan forward. His aim was to gain some recognition from one of the terrorist groups that he was told was operating in Australia. Originally, he had intended to kidnap a bus full of kids and hold them until he was able to make the necessary contacts. Dizzy believed that his actions would bring attention to the terrible things Westerners were doing to people in the Muslim world. Exactly what these things were, Dizzy wasn't sure. At times, it seemed to him to be the other way round. Once he had gained the attention he was seeking, he would release his hostages and hope that the authorities would not be too harsh on him.

But now there would be one crucial change to his plan. Instead of kidnapping a bus full of kids, he would take the sixteen bowlers hostage.

Dizzy knew he had the persuasive power needed to control the situation. He reached under his bed and pulled out a box of religious books. Secreted between two of the books was a replica pistol. He turned the weapon over in his hand, and the feel of cold steel made him shudder. Dizzy was not a violent man.

Dizzy had located an abandoned shed in the hills just off the Pacific Highway, near Mullumbimby. It was impossible to see the shed from the dirt road leading to the building, so he could hold the group there for several days without being discovered. He would contact the media and tell them what he had done, then demand a meeting with one of the local terrorist groups to explain his actions.

For the first time in his life, the young man was overwhelmed with a strong sense of power. Soon, he told himself, people would begin to take notice of Dizzy Abood.

Chapter Seventeen

Penny Applebee and Clarissa van Hooganband stood at the entrance to Serenity Quays, waiting for the bus. Despite Penny's disturbing encounter with Mabel Munzie a few weeks earlier, she had persisted with her practice, and was beginning to enjoy her lawn bowls. And this was a bowls trip both she and Clarissa were looking forward to. Like the others who were milling around the bus stop, there was a great deal of interest in a visit to Hideaway Cove. Few of them had been inside the resort, and a number wanted to inspect the place that would soon be their new home. Of the thirty people planning to join the excursion, many had never played lawn bowls in their life.

"The people from the bus company say there's only sixteen seats available," Quinsy Naylor called to the group as they waited for their transport to arrive. "Some of you will have to stay behind."

"We'll stand," someone yelled.

"Standing is not permitted," Quinsy said. He was enjoying his role as decision maker.

Quinsy took a slip of paper from his pocket and checked his list. "This trip is for the lawn bowlers, so only the following people will be allowed to join the bus." Quinsy began reading out the sixteen names. Most of them were his drinking mates from the sports club, and their wives.

"Willy Hogan and Gill Tucker aren't bowlers," Penny called out loudly.

"They're gonna start learning today," Arty Bullpit mumbled.

"But Clarissa and I put our names down for this trip last week, and there were seats available." Penny took a deep breath— she rarely became this angry. "We demand that you give us our seats," she shouted.

Quinsy fiddled nervously with his slip of paper, unable to decide the best course of action. It was Gill Tucker who rescued him from an embarrassing situation. "Give the ladies our seats, Quinsy. We'll see the resort some other time."

By the time the mini-bus arrived, the passenger list had been decided, and the group was prepared to leave for Hideaway Cove.

* * *

Dizzy was extremely nervous as the bus began its one-hour trip to their planned destination. Apart from an unpleasant man named Bullpit, who took an immediate dislike to Dizzy, the mood of the passengers was friendly. Two nice ladies named Penny and Clarissa sat in the front seat behind Dizzy and chattered amicably with him as they set off.

The group soon began singing songs with strange lyrics, which made no sense to Dizzy. He found himself fascinated by this odd collection of people, particularly the pretty lady named Penny. Dizzy observed her in his rear view mirror as she led the sing-along. Her beautiful voice was not unlike the woman called *Maria Callas*, whom his mother listened to on her old record player. She leant forward and smiled at him. "Why don't you sing along with us, driver?" she said.

At first Dizzy was reluctant to participate, but as he listened, he was captivated by the lilting melody of their song. *When Irish hearts are happy, all the world seems bright and gay...* A peculiar song, Dizzy thought, singing about queers, but the words were uncomplicated, and Dizzy, with a good ear for a tune and a pleasant voice, had little difficulty joining in.

It seemed strange how the atmosphere inside the bus lifted his spirits, while the mini-bus seemed to glide along the highway. *...In the lilt of Irish laughter, you can hear the angels sing.* As a child, singing was the only thing Dizzy did well. But when he was fourteen, his voice broke. Whenever he sang after that, his father would say, "Now you sound like an old bull frog, Dizzy," and everyone would laugh. Dizzy was humiliated by the ridicule, so eventually he had stopped singing altogether. Now, for the first time in years, he suddenly felt the urge to sing again, and the feeling was wonderful.

When the singing stopped for a moment, Penny leant forward and patted Dizzy on the shoulder. "What's your name, driver?" she asked.

"Adisi," he said, "but everyone calls me Dizzy."

"Well, sing us a song you know, Dizzy," Penny said.

Dizzy looked up into the rear view mirror and saw everyone watching him. "I used to sing a song in church, when I was a kid," he said, flushing with embarrassment. "That's the only one I know."

"We don't want any hymns on this bus trip, thanks, Dizzy," Quinsy Naylor yelled, then laughed mockingly at him.

"Don't listen to him," Penny said, leaning forward again and smiling at him. "Sing your song for us, Dizzy."

Dizzy cleared his throat, then he began singing *Ave Maria*. The bus fell silent as Dizzy was carried back to the days when he sang in the school choir. To the days when the dulcet sounds of his young soprano voice would echo around the walls of the local church, causing his mother and grandmother to weep with joy. When the congregation would marvel at the sweetness and purity of his voice. A time when even his father would nod in approval at his son's unmistakable talent. As his confidence grew, Dizzy found a new voice that seemed more powerful and resilient. Now, notes that were strained when he was a child resonated like thunder in the confines of the tiny bus.

A blast from a car horn shattered the air, and, for a moment, Dizzy was unsure where he was. He looked down and saw that he was travelling below the speed limit, and there was a build-up of traffic behind him. Not that it was worrying his passengers—they had burst into noisy cheers and more loud applause.

As he picked up speed, Dizzy checked his bearings. Then he gasped with dismay. He was so preoccupied with his singing, he had driven straight past his turn-off to the old shed. Dizzy was confused as he removed his foot from the accelerator and the mini-bus came to a halt beside the highway.

Stopping for a pee are we, Dizzy?" Quinsy Naylor called from the back of the bus, causing his mates to burst into laughter.

"Nah, he's lost. He can't find the Pacific Highway," Arty Bullpit responded, and laughed raucously.

The laughter continued as Dizzy glared back at the rear view mirror. He hated them all, always ridiculing, always laughing at him. Those cruel, nasty insults—you're too fat, Dizzy; you're too hairy, Dizzy; you're ugly, Dizzy. Cruel, unkind remarks like his father made. You're lazy, and you can't do anything because you're *stupid*, Dizzy. The word seemed to resonate through his brain—*stupid, stupid, stupid.*

Dizzy looked at the sign where he had parked by the side of the road. Off to the left was the town of Billinudgel, so he had gone only a few kilometres past his turn-off. He could go through the town and take a back route, which would lead him to his dirt road, and the shed.

Dizzy was still deciding what he should do when Penny leant forward. "Are you okay, love?" she asked. "If you don't get going, we'll be late for our bowls match."

Dizzy turned to face Penny. Something about the woman reminded him of his mother. He smiled when he thought of his mother—at least *she* wasn't mean to him.

"Come on, Dizzy, get your Arab finger out," Arty Bullpit called out loudly.

Dizzy looked at the man in the rear view mirror and a feeling of hatred overwhelmed him. Right, he said to himself. That's it, you bastard; this bus has just been hijacked. Dizzy angrily slammed the vehicle into gear and turned off the highway.

"Where the bloody hell are we going?" Naylor asked.

"We're taking the scenic route," Dizzy replied abruptly.

Within ten minutes, Dizzy was lost. He recognised none of the landmarks, while the road he was on seemed to be taking them further from the highway. When the sealed road narrowed into a dirt track, the mood of his passengers began to change—they were becoming restless. Soon, Dizzy would have to show his hand. He reached under his seat and felt the revolver that he had hidden there. He had turned away for just a moment, and when he looked up, he cried out in dismay. The dirt road had suddenly come to an end. In front of him was a scenic lookout on a steep hillside.

Dizzy parked the bus, then got up from the driver's seat and stood facing his passengers. He raised himself to his full height, his large frame blocking out the front of the vehicle. "This bus has been hijacked," he said loudly, endeavouring to engender as much authority in his voice as possible. "You're now my hostages."

There was silence for a moment, then someone laughed.

"Christ, one minute he's Pavarotti, next he's Osama bin Ladin," Stan Huddle yelled, and laughter broke out throughout the bus.

Only Penny Applebee showed any signs of alarm; everyone else seemed to think it was some sort of prank. As his passengers continued to laugh and mock him, Dizzy's anger grew. This is how it always was. These people were being kidnapped, and everyone, except the two nice ladies in the front, was treating it as a joke. He bent down and took the pistol from under his seat, then raised it in the air. The pistol hit the roof of the bus with a thud, and the laughter began to abate. There was a nervous giggle, and then the bus fell silent.

"Everyone out of the bus," Dizzy demanded, as he switched on his mobile phone.

He had no idea how often tourists visited the lookout, so he needed to make his contact with the media quickly. He had listed the number of an ethnic newspaper in Sydney run by people he was sure would make the necessary contacts on his behalf.

When Dizzy checked his phone, he whimpered softly—there was no phone signal on the isolated hillside. He wouldn't be able to use his mobile phone to ring the newspaper. He looked up and saw that everyone was watching him with amused expressions on their faces.

"So what are you gonna do now, mate?" Clarry Humphries asked in a sarcastic tone. "Demand a million dollar ransom for our release?"

"If you do, we want half," Marty Fisk responded.

There was more laughter, and Dizzy's anger grew. He raised the pistol in the air as if he were going to fire a warning shot. At that moment, Penny stepped forward and turned to the crowd. "Why don't you all shut up for a minute so we can get to the bottom of this."

She walked over to Dizzy and put her arm on his shoulder. Her action alarmed Clarissa, who cried out to her. "Penny, be careful, he has a gun."

Penny ignored the warning and spoke softly to Dizzy. "Why are you doing this Dizzy—what are you trying to prove?" she asked.

"Give him a kiss, gorgeous, and then we can get on our way," Willy Hogan yelled loudly.

Clarissa turned towards Hogan, unable to contain her anger. "Shut your bloody mouth, Willy Hogan, or I'll come over there and deal with you myself." There was murmur of surprise from the group. No one had ever heard Clarissa Van Hooganband speak with such authority before.

At that moment, Dizzy cried out in despair, then he suddenly went limp. The whole ridiculous escapade had become too much for him. He was no terrorist—he was nothing, a weakling masquerading as a radical extremist. His heroic attempt to gain notoriety had been a charade.

"I just want people to respect me," he said, and collapsed on his knees, weeping like a child.

Penny knelt down and held the young man in her arms, the gun in Dizzy's hands resting on her shoulder.

"That gun isn't real, it's a replica," Arty Bullpit said, shuffling forward a few paces to take a closer look at the weapon. "Look at the barrel; it's solid. The frigging thing is a toy."

"Is that right, Dizzy? Is the gun only a replica?" Penny asked.

Dizzy hung his head, his shame now beginning to overwhelm him. "Yes," he whimpered softly.

Penny took hold of the gun by the barrel, and Dizzy let his arm fall limply to the ground. Holding the gun at a distance between her thumb and forefinger, Penny went to the edge of the escarpment and, with all the strength she could muster, hurled it out into space. The weapon seemed to sit suspended in mid air for a moment, then it dropped away, making a weird whirring sound as it plunged into the rugged bush below.

When Penny turned, she saw Bullpit rush from behind the bus with a large tree branch, brandishing it above his head. Penny cried out a warning to the young man, who was still squatting on the ground. Dizzy heard Penny's cry and looked up into the oncoming face of Bullpit, his eyes wide with hatred. Then Dizzy did an amazing thing. Like a gazelle, he sprang to one side and rolled skilfully out of harm's way. The momentum of Bullpit's charge, and his vicious blow, thrust him forward with such force that he stumbled onwards for a few metres, tripped on a safety barrier, then disappeared over the edge of the hillside.

Before anyone could react, Dizzy ran to the edge, dropped onto his stomach, and looked over into the void below. "Help me," he called. "Someone hold my legs."

Bert Pugh and Clarry Humphries grabbed Dizzy—one on each ankle. Those who could get close enough watched in horror as Dizzy gripped Bullpit by his arm. He had snagged himself on a small wattle tree growing out of the rocks. It was the only thing between Bullpit and a 500-metre drop into the valley below. Slowly, Dizzy dragged Bullpit up into his arms, then held him tightly as the men pulled them both to safety.

As Dizzy and Bullpit sat huddled together on the ground, trying to regain their composure, Penny Applebee turned to her fellow passengers. "Do I have everyone's agreement that nothing happened here today?" she asked, looking around the group.

It was Quinsy Naylor who broke the silence. "I think I've had enough *sightseeing* for today. How about we all go home?"

The homeward journey began sedately, with the passengers talking quietly amongst themselves about the morning's strange events. Everyone on the bus agreed that, regardless of Dizzy Abood's bravery, risking his life to rescue Arty Bullpit, the incident must remain a secret. The bowls tournament and the inspection of their new home no longer seemed important, so it was agreed that the visit to Hideaway Cove should be abandoned.

By the time Dizzy had the mini-bus back to the highway, the incident seemed almost forgotten. As the bus turned south and headed back towards Serenity Quays, everyone on board was in full voice once again. Even Arty Bullpit joined the chorus as they sang along with Dizzy Abood.

When Irish hearts are happy, all the world seems bright and gay...

Chapter Eighteen

Mort Fiddlemore moved uneasily in his chair as the lawyer flicked through the contract. Davenport's corporate lawyers had summoned him to their Gold Coast office to resolve a possible hitch in the sale of Serenity Quays.

"My client wishes to add a clause to the final draft of the contract." The lawyer looked at Fiddlemore over the top of his glasses. "It's a rider covering land usage in the event of flooding."

Fiddlemore relaxed immediately. Serenity Quays has never been flooded, so what was this clown on about?

"If you feel it's important, go ahead," he replied.

"So your client won't have any objections if we add such a clause?"

"Why should he? There's never been any flooding in the ten years the site has been occupied. And, besides, the land was passed by Council as suitable for residential development."

"Very well, Mr. Fiddlemore. If you feel your client will be happy with the added rider, we'll go ahead and sign the formal contract."

A few minutes after leaving the lawyer's office, Fiddlemore rang Dermot Bollinger on his mobile phone.

"I didn't bother calling you earlier, Dermot. The whole thing was a furphy. They just wanted to add a rider about flooding on the site.

"What did you tell them?" His question was terse.

"I said there were no problems with floodwaters in Serenity Quays, so I told them to go ahead and add the clause." Suddenly, Fiddlemore felt uneasy. "There aren't any problems with flooding, are there, Dermot?"

"No, no problems, Mort," he said, a little vaguely.

After he finished the call with Fiddlemore, Bollinger sat back in his chair and rubbed his chin. Could Davenport have found out about the recent flooding at Serenity Quays? And if he did, from whom? There was no one at Serenity Quays who knew Davenport Developments were the buyers—only he, his solicitors, and Fiddlemore had access to that information. No, he thought, and shook his head. Davenport and his lawyers are just being cautious.

* * *

The day following the bus trip, Penny rang the number Dizzy had given her. She had made several phone calls about a singing audition for Dizzy, and she needed him to be prepared.

"Mr. Abood, my name's Penny Applebee," she said when Dizzy's father answered the phone. "I was on a bus your son was driving yesterday."

"Yeah, he never stopped talkin' about you last night. What are you up to lady? Are you tryin' to get your hands on my son?"

"What do you mean?" Penny asked, knowing exactly what the man meant.

"You know, racing the kid off. I've heard about you older women."

"Hardly, Mr. Abood. I have a daughter older than Dizzy." She hesitated. "Would it be better if I spoke to Mrs. Abood?" she asked. There was a hint of acrimony in her voice.

"If you got something to say about my son, you say it to me," he replied.

Penny sighed and shook her head. "Dizzy was singing for us on the bus yesterday. He has a wonderful voice, don't you agree, Mr. Abood?"

There was silence for a moment. "Dizzy doesn't sing no more," he replied abruptly. It was obvious to Penny that Abood hadn't heard his son singing for some time.

"Well, I think he has loads of talent, and I'd like to send him to a friend of mine who could help him get a singing career started."

"Singing career," Abood shouted angrily. "Dizzy doesn't want no career. He works for me; he's a bus driver."

Through the phone, Penny heard loud voices arguing, then a thumping sound as if someone had dropped the receiver. "Hello, this is Sophy Abood speaking," a woman said. "Are you the nice lady that…that helped Dizzy yesterday?" she asked.

Penny was relieved to be rid of the father. "Yes I am, Sophy, my name is Penny."

She cleared her throat. "I'm sorry for what my husband say to you, he's a very rude man," she said loudly, as much a chastisement for her husband as an apology to Penny.

"Did you know that Dizzy is keen to pursue a singing career, Sophy?" Penny asked.

"We talk about it last night." There was excitement in the woman's voice. "He says he wants to sing opera—do you think my Dizzy sings good enough to be opera singer?"

"I was in the entertainment business for thirty years, Sophy. I think I know talent when I hear it."

"Okay, you go ahead and make the arrangements, Penny, and I'll make sure Dizzy does everything you ask."

"Your son is a nice young man, Sophy, he deserves a chance."

"You and me, Penny, we give him that chance, right?"

"Right, Sophy. I'll call you in a few days."

Chapter Nineteen

For the first time since Serenity Quays was established, almost every resident was in attendance for the Annual General Meeting and the election of their committee. For the few unable to attend, proxy vote forms had been signed, ensuring that the elections, for this year at least, would be well contested.

Quinsy Naylor looked around the room nervously as the clubhouse filled to capacity and the call went out for more chairs. There had never been an attendance like this at any previous AGM, and he was worried. In the past, complacency had always assisted in his re-election, as the majority of the residents failed to realise, or were indifferent to, the way Bollinger's mob manipulated the voting. Most residents were unaware how far Quinsy Naylor's friends would go to ensure that he was elected chairman of the Tenants' Committee, and one of their own was chosen as secretary. Buffy Bullpit, the current secretary, also expressed alarm as the noisy crowd settled in for the meeting.

Buffy looked around the hall. "I don't like the look of this," she said. "Arty had a feeling those *Category 4* lot were up to something."

"Well, let's get the meeting under way before any more turn up," Naylor replied, as he searched for the meeting's agenda.

The preliminary matters out of the way, Quinsy announced that he and the secretary would stand down, and elections would be held for office bearers for the next twelve months. "Buffy and I will stand for re-election," he said confidently. There was a rousing, *"here, here"* from the two front rows, where Bollinger's mob always gathered during tenant meetings. "As we have no other nominations, I'll declare the positions filled," Quinsy said, and smiled—obviously relieved that the election of office bearers had been successfully resolved.

"Point of order, Mr. Chairperson. I'd like to nominate for the position of chairman of the Tenants' Committee."

The crowd turned to where Tony Bloom stood with his hand raised, holding his nomination form.

"And I wish to nominate for the secretary's position."

A loud murmur filled the room as Sissy Witherspoon rose to her feet, also holding a nomination form.

Quinsy squirmed in his chair. "This is most irregular," he said, looking towards Spencer J. Scraggs. "We had no, um… warning… that anyone else was interested in running for the positions."

"That's not relevant, Mr. Chairperson. Our nominations must be accepted," Tony Bloom said, as he turned towards the assemblage, who were enjoying the exciting contest that was now unfolding.

"No they don't. You were asked to have your nomination forms in two weeks before today's meeting," Buffy Bullpit shouted.

"Why?" the Major said, jumping to his feet. "So you'd have the time to undermine anyone who opposed you?"

A loud supportive cheer arose from around the room.

"May I make a brief comment, Mr. Chairperson?"

It was Spencer J. Scraggs who slowly rose from his chair. An audible sigh went up from the room. Many residents had been victims of Scraggs' *brief comments* in the past, and most found him an insufferable bore. "Sit down you silly old fart," someone called from the back of the room.

Scraggs ignored the comment, and, for the next thirty minutes, rambled on about government regulations and the proper procedures for the election of office bearers. This was an old tactic of Scraggs'. He had often risen to the defence of Naylor when, through the man's own ignorance and stupidity, he had landed himself in an awkward situation. Scraggs could bore an audience for long periods with his irrelevant prattle, so that, in the end, arguments were quashed simply because Naylor's detractors gave up in frustration—or the meeting disintegrated in boredom and confusion.

"My understanding is that nominations should have been in prior to the meeting…"

Scraggs was just getting warmed up when he was interrupted. "I have a copy of the regulations here, Mr. Scraggs, and there's nothing to prevent a resident nominating for the committee at the AGM." Charles Badminton-Smyth stood holding the lengthy document in his hand.

"Sit down, Scraggs, and let's get on with the election," someone called from the floor.

Quinsy again looked to Scraggs for guidance as he took his seat, but Scraggs shrugged and turned away. Quinsy spoke quietly to his secretary, and she nodded. He turned back to the meeting. "As chairman of the Tenants' Committee, I feel I have no alternative but to terminate this AGM so the matter of late nominations can be fully investigated."

"You can't do that, it's unconstitutional," Penny Applebee shouted angrily.

"As the chairman of the Tenants' Committee, he can do what he likes," Arty Bullpit shouted back.

"He's no longer the chairman, Bullpit," the Major said, glaring at Arty. "He and his secretary just stood down. At this point in time, there's no Tenants' Committee." The Major turned to the meeting. "I move that the elections continue as required by the regulations."

"I second that motion," Gerry Curry called loudly.

Quinsy looked towards Scraggs in desperation, but Scraggs was deep in conversation with another tenant. He wiped the perspiration from his brow and looked around the angry faces in the room—there was no alternative. "All those in favour of the elections proceeding immediately?" he asked tentatively.

Buffy Bullpit didn't bother counting the show of hands. At least two thirds of the tenants voted in favour of the elections proceeding.

A wild flurry of activity followed, as residents, scrutineers, and nominees mingled together. An hour later, a hush descended on the room as the results were handed to Naylor by one of the scrutineers. Quinsy's face reddened as he stared, open-mouthed, at the slip of paper. He was hardly audible as he called the results. "The elected secretary of the Tenants' Committee, with 59 votes…Sissy Witherspoon." A loud cheer went up from the room. "Elected chairman of the Tenants' Committee, with 63 votes…" Quinsy choked and appeared on the brink of tears. "Tony Bloom," he said, just loud enough for those in the front two rows to hear.

The Major raised his hand and, above the commotion, shouted loudly, "Point of order, Mr. Chairperson, we couldn't hear you. Would you repeat the election results for the position of chairman on our new Tenants' Committee, please?"

Rising a little unsteadily to his feet, and in an emotional voice, Quinsy answered weakly, "Tony Bloom is now the chairman of the Tenants' Committee."

Quinsy gathered his things from the table and, amidst sustained applause from the floor for the successful candidates, he hurried from the clubhouse.

As Tony Bloom watched Quinsy leave through a side door of the building, he couldn't help feeling a little sorry for the man he was replacing.

* * *

"How could you allow this to happen?" Dermot Bollinger asked the two men sitting opposite him. "Now we've lost control of the residents." Bollinger, Scraggs, and Bullpit were sitting in Felicity Grimes' lounge room, discussing the results of the previous day's Annual General Meeting.

"It was a set up," Bullpit said, passing the results of the elections across the coffee table to Bollinger. "That bunch of arse holes kept Bloom's nomination a secret until the meeting."

Bollinger stubbed his cigar into the ashtray. "That's not what I hear, Arty. It seems they were canvassing Tony Bloom's nomination weeks ago. They also did a selective door knock the night before. Your group were the only ones that didn't know about it."

"Well, it's too late to do anything now. Witherspoon and Bloom are running the committee," Scraggs said, as he slumped disconsolately in one of Felicity's large lounge chairs.

"We'll need to make sure a new Tenants' Committee is formed for stage two of Hideaway Cove when your lot gets there," Bollinger said. "And I want someone on the committee that I can manipulate—someone like that idiot Naylor."

"Maybe Bloom could have an accident," Bullpit suggested, and smirked.

"A nice thought, Arty," Bollinger said, glancing casually at the election figures, "but that might be a little too radical. No, I have a better idea. We'll begin moving our own people to Hideaway Cove first—you, Naylor, all your drinking mates, and everyone else from our side. When we have the numbers, we'll call a special meeting to form a *new* Tenants' Committee. If Bloom and Witherspoon are still here at Serenity Quays, they can't be on the committee of stage two at Hideaway Cove."

Bollinger sat back in his chair, feeling rather pleased with himself, and blew a perfectly formed smoke ring into the air.

"That's a brilliant idea," Bullpit remarked.

Scraggs looked thoughtful for a moment. "Yes, but is it constitutional?" he asked.

"Fuck the constitution," Bollinger replied, rummaging through a bundle of signed agreements. "Now, how many residents have agreed to move to Hideaway Cove?"

"Fifty-five tenants have signed, and another fifteen or so have indicated that they will after they speak with their families or solicitors." Scraggs checked his notes. "A few are still undecided whether to come with us or go to another park. We understand nine tenants are planning to sell their homes and move back into the community. It appears that only one tenant is refusing to leave."

"They don't have a choice. Everyone has to move—give me a name," Bollinger snapped.

"An old guy named Albert Titmus. He's a widower, and a real loony—one of the first tenants to buy into Serenity Quays."

Arty Bullpit rubbed his nose. "The house is one of the early demountables with two bedrooms. Looks in poor condition, but it's sitting on the point near the lake, probably the best building site in the estate."

"Ah yes, Titmus—suffers from dementia, I believe. His family wants him in a nursing home, probably so they can get their hands on his money. They asked Grimes to list his house for sale." Bollinger got to his feet and began pacing the floor. "We'll offer his family, say, fifty grand. Far more than the house is worth. In return, they have the old bastard committed to a nursing home, and out of our hair."

"Fifty grand, Dermot? It's not worth fifteen," Scraggs exclaimed. "It wouldn't even pay to move it from the site."

"So we'll bulldoze the place. Hell, this is working out better than I'd planned. Only one difficult tenant out of eighty-five—it's worth fifty grand."

"How soon do you want our group packed and ready to go?" Bullpit asked.

"Within a month. There're twenty-five homes now under construction, and some of these will be ready for occupation within two weeks. Most of the homes here at Serenity Quays will be dismantled and taken to Hideaway Cove—the rest will be sent to our resort at Port Macquarie." Bollinger continued to pace the floor. "We estimate that the ninety homes planned for stage two will be on site and tenanted within five months. I want Serenity Quays to be a vacant site when settlement occurs in six months time."

Scraggs and Bullpit looked at one another in amazement. The speed with which their boss worked was astounding. "Anything else, Dermot?" Scraggs asked, getting to his feet.

"Yes, Spencer, there is. I want you to consider running for the chairman's position on the new committee."

As they prepared to leave, Felicity Grimes moved away from her closed lounge room door, where she'd been listening to the men's conversation. When Bollinger entered the office, she was sitting at her desk.

"Felicity, your back?" he said, looking a little embarrassed. "I hope you don't mind—the boys and I have been having a little chat in your lounge room."

Chapter Twenty

Tony Bloom and Sissy Witherspoon had called an emergency meeting to discuss Bollinger's plans to sell Serenity Quays. Because of the important matters being discussed, almost every resident was present. Dermot Bollinger had insisted that he be allowed to attend, and had already begun to dominate the proceedings. Bollinger was determined not to let this one get out of his control.

"We appreciate your offer to move us to your resort on the Tweed Coast, Mr. Bollinger, but what is there at Hideaway Cove that we don't have at Serenity Quays?" Sissy Witherspoon looked across to Bollinger, who was sitting at an adjoining table with Felicity Grimes. "Given a choice, most of the residents don't want to go through the upheaval of packing up and moving to a new area. We're happy living here. If we have to get out because Serenity Quays is being sold, we see no reason why we should have to pay for that inconvenience and disruption to our lives."

"That's nonsense," Quinsy Naylor shouted. "We're quite happy with the proposal Mr. Bollinger has put forward."

Tony Bloom ignored Naylor's comments. "What we are saying, Mr. Bollinger, is that we don't believe the residents should be out of pocket because you've decided to sell Serenity Quays. What we're recommending, on behalf of the residents moving to Hideaway Cove, is that they be moved there by your organisation, free of charge." Tony cleared his throat, then continued. "We also believe that those wishing to move elsewhere should be paid your current list price for their homes—plus a relocation allowance of five thousand dollars."

"You can't be serious, Mr. Bloom. Do you think we're made of money? Your demands are totally unacceptable," Bollinger replied, waving his arms in a dramatic show of indignation. "This is a business enterprise, not a charitable institution."

"Mr. Bollinger, we believe our demands, as you call them, are more than reasonable when you consider the huge profit you'll be making from the sale of this resort."

Bollinger studied the face of the person who had just spoken from the floor, and he suddenly felt uneasy. He had seen the man recently in another place—but where?

"How dare you speak that way to Mr. Bollinger. This's the reason you weren't elected to the committee last year, Curry. You're a troublemaker." Quinsy Naylor pointed an accusing finger at Gerry. "I believe you owe Mr. Bollinger an apology," he said.

"I agree, Mr. Chairman. I also object to Mr. Curry's statement." Now it was Spencer J. Scraggs' turn to undermine the comments made by the person who had dared to question their *leader.* He and Naylor had developed a strategy whereby they attacked their adversaries in tandem during their meetings. "The profit Mr. Bollinger's company makes is none of our business," he said in an officious tone.

A rowdy, "*here, here"* went up from Bollinger's mob in the front row.

Gerry Curry rose to his feet again. "The residents of Serenity Quays are being thrown out of their homes and forced to resettle into a totally new environment in order to facilitate the sale of this resort. Now your organisation wants to impose a costly fee on the residents to make this unwanted move. Under the circumstances, I believe the residents have every right to know what financial gain you'll realise from the sale of Serenity Quays, Mr. Bollinger."

"Mr. Curry," Bollinger said, with a wave of his hand and a friendly smile, "I can assure you that after we've moved everyone from Serenity Quays to Hideaway Cove, the profit I make from the sale of this resort will be very modest—very modest indeed."

"I would hardly call the figures I've seen modest, Mr. Bollinger." Gerry looked thoughtful for a moment. "On the contrary, I would say that the profit you stand to make is quite staggering."

A loud murmur erupted from the floor as Spencer J. Scraggs rose to his feet again and began to speak. "Mr. Chairman, I suggest that Mr. Curry's comments are offensive, and he should be ejected from this meeting."

Bollinger studied Curry closely, and his uneasiness continued. Where had he seen the man before? Then his confidence rose. What would he know, anyway? The deal was to remain confidential, even after settlement, and only he and Fiddlemore and the directors at Davenport Developments knew the details of the transaction. Let this troublemaker make a fool of himself, he thought.

"No, Mr. Chairman." Bollinger turned towards Tony Bloom and smiled. "Mr. Curry seems to have some fascinating information that even I am unaware of." There was laughter from the front row. "I think he should be allowed to put his misguided opinions to the meeting today so that I can challenge them in public. After all, this's still a democratic country, and a reputable businessman like myself should take every opportunity to defend himself, even against the most outrageous rumours and accusations."

Bollinger's mob broke into sustained clapping and more "*here, heres.*"

Gerry Curry rose to his feet and removed several documents from his jacket pocket as an eerie silence settled over the room. "Mr. Chairman," he said softly, "because of my business interests, I sometimes come across development projects that are confidential, and highly sensitive. Normally, I would never divulge such information publicly." Gerry looked around the room. "For that reason, I'm most reluctant to pass on certain confidential information that has come into my possession regarding the sale of Serenity Quays. While Mr. Bollinger has no objection to this information becoming public, I'm concerned for the rights of the other party." Gerry held up the documents. "But this information concerns everyone here today, and I believe I have an obligation to give you a brief summary, at least, of the details concerning the sale of Serenity Quays."

Dermot Bollinger shifted uncomfortably in his chair. Impossible, he thought. There's no way this weasel could have acquired such information. He's just a resident of Serenity Quays—one of his own tenants, for Christ's sake.

Gerry opened the documents in his hand and began reading. "This is an interim agreement whereby Vertigo Properties, a division of Bollinger Investments Pty Ltd, agrees to sell the Residential Resort known as Serenity Quays to Davenport Developments for the sum of 22.5 million dollars. This contract is subject to vacant possession of the land within six months from the above date of this agreement and is subject to the following conditions…"

Bollinger jumped to his feet, sending his chair clattering to the ground. "Where did you get those documents? That information's confidential!" he shouted.

Gerry Curry ignored Bollinger's outburst and held up a second and equally important looking document towards the audience. "There was also a formal application from Davenport Developments to Council, requesting that the land now occupied by Serenity Quays as a Residential Park Estate be rezoned for high-density residential development…"

Bollinger moved to the edge of the podium and raised a clenched fist at Gerry. He had now lost all semblance of self-control. "You'll pay for this, Curry, or whatever your name is." He turned, then angrily grabbed his coat from the upturned chair and flung it over his shoulder. As he did so, the coat dragged his hairpiece over his forehead, leaving him, as the Major was later to recall, looking remarkably like Mo, of The Three Stooges.

A ripple of muffled laughter rose from the meeting as Bollinger stormed out the door, closely followed, a few seconds later, by Felicity Grimes.

It was a question from Charles Badminton-Smyth that brought the meeting back to order. "Mr. Chairman, I believe we've had enough comment from the floor. Can we hear your committee's recommendations in full, please?"

"Certainly, Charles," Tony replied, and cleared his throat. "The Tenants' Committee proposes that the following motion be put to Management in order to facilitate the amicable and speedy closure of Serenity Quays. 'All residents transferring from Serenity Quays to Hideaway Cove are to be moved by the owner free of any entry fee or removal charges. The weekly rental charges will also remain unchanged with increases linked to the national CPI. The owners moving to Hideaway Cove will also be seeking a twenty-year lease on their land. Residents that do not wish to relocate to Hideaway Cove will be paid the company's current list price for their houses, plus a five thousand dollar relocation allowance.'"

"I find that motion to be absolutely absurd, Mr. Chairman," Spencer J. Scraggs exclaimed loudly. "Do you have any idea what it would cost Mr. Bollinger's organisation if they agreed to such a claim?"

"Given that Mr. Bollinger owns his own furniture removalist and house moving businesses, his cost will probably be around a million dollars." All eyes had once again turned to Gerry Curry, who was enjoying his role of devil's advocate. "He'll dismantle and transport the vacated homes by his freight company, at minimal cost, some to his new resort in Port Macquarie, where he'll no doubt make a handsome profit when he sells them again." Gerry withdrew a notebook from his pocket, then flicked over the pages. "I did some figures last night, and I estimate that Mr. Bollinger's costs to remove his tenants from Serenity Quays would be less than three hundred thousand dollars. Allowing another seven hundred thousand dollars to dismantle and relocate the vacated homes, I reckon Mr. Bollinger stands to make a substantial profit from this sale, Mr. Scraggs."

Scraggs was unable to respond for a moment—Curry's estimates were reasonably accurate. "How would *you* know what Mr. Bollinger's costs were on a project of this scale?" he asked scornfully.

"What I do know, Mr. Scraggs, is that your friend Bollinger gained control of Serenity Quays for a mere two hundred thousand dollars. Now, eight years later, he's selling the resort for more than twenty-two million—that's a net profit of more than twenty-one million dollars in my estimation. Under the circumstances, I believe it would be immoral for Mr. Bollinger *not* to accept our motion."

A loud cheer went up from the floor, and Charles Badminton-Smyth called loudly above the din. "I would like to second the motion put forward by Tony Bloom."

* * *

That afternoon the action group met on Tony's verandah. They all sat quietly, reflecting on the morning's events—each prepared to give an opinion on the success or failure of their meeting.

"You really nailed the bastard with those documents, Gerry. How did you manage to get hold of them?" the Major asked.

"No problem, really," Gerry replied, removing them from his coat pocket and placing them on the table.

Tony Bloom inspected the two documents, then looked at Gerry in disbelief. "But this's your last rate notice, and this…this thing is a letter about a free bowel cancer test," he said.

"So?" Gerry replied.

"You crazy son of a bitch," Evy Bloom muttered quietly.

"You're a fool, Gerry Curry. You'll be crucified if Bollinger and his cronies find out what you did." Sue Curry was annoyed by her husband's reckless behaviour.

"I think the man's a hero," Penny Applebee responded. "If Sue throws you out, Gerry, you can come around to my place. I need some excitement in my life."

Tony Bloom glared at Gerry. "What if I'd asked you to table the documents for the meeting's records?"

Gerry shrugged. "But you didn't, did you? Besides, I'd seen the actual documents, so I committed the wording to memory. I was sure that we'd get the reaction we did from Bollinger when I quoted the details."

"Well, I think it was a brilliant tactic—it's given us the upper hand," the Major said confidently. "Almost everyone voted in favour of the motion, even some of Bollinger's mob."

The phone rang and Evy went to answer it.

"So, what do we do now?" Sue asked.

"Sit back and wait for Bollinger to respond to the motion, and pray that he doesn't throw us all out into the street," Tony replied.

"Well you're not going to wait long," Evy said from the doorway. "Bollinger wants to meet with you and Sissy to discuss your proposal before he leaves."

* * *

"I've considered your request, and there are a number of points that are unacceptable. In fact , some of them are ridiculous, and not even negotiable," Bollinger said, as he shuffled through some papers.

Tony and Sissy sat opposite Bollinger, who had taken over Felicity's desk. She stood in the background watching the proceedings, a mildly amused expression on her face. It seemed to Tony that Felicity was reluctant to become involved in the negotiations.

"They're not my requests, Mr. Bollinger. It's a motion supported by ninety percent of the residents," Tony replied.

"Mr. Bloom, you may have coerced the other residents into voting for your demands, but I'm telling you now, most of them are out of the question." Bollinger picked up the committee's motion, then cast a dismissive hand over the document. "I'm not paying full price for second-hand homes, and the five thousand dollar allowance is out of the question—so is the twenty-year lease."

Bollinger threw his copy of the committee's motion on the desk and glared threateningly at Tony and Sissy.

"It's a pity you feel that way, Mr. Bollinger, because now you leave us no alternative," Tony said, picking up his mobile phone and dialling a number.

Bollinger laughed. "And whom are you calling?" he asked.

"We have someone on stand-by at the local television station, Mr. Bollinger. We've been asked to do an interview for the evening news. We'll also be handing over certain documents during that interview." Tony finished dialling the number, maintaining eye contact with Bollinger as he spoke. "Hello, Gerry, this is Tony. I'm sorry mate, but you're going on air. Mr. Bollinger has rejected our proposal."

"Wait!" Bollinger bellowed so loudly that Felicity jumped. "Is that Curry on the line?" Bollinger was having difficulty controlling his anger.

"Yes it is," Tony replied.

"Does that bastard have any idea who he's dealing with?" Bollinger shouted.

"Oh, Gerry knows more about you than you realise, Mr. Bollinger," Sissy said.

Bollinger slammed his fist on Felicity's desk. "All right then, I accept your contemptible motion, but on one condition—Curry has to go. I don't want him living in any of my resorts. I'll pay him full price for his house, including the five thousand dollar subsidy—just get him out of my life."

"Did you hear that, Gerry?" Tony asked. He listened for a moment, then ended the call.

Tony smiled at Bollinger. "Gerry said to tell you he'll ring a removalist immediately after he gets off the phone."

Less than a hundred metres away, Gerry Curry put away his phone. He was sitting on the Major's verandah with Sue and Jessie, sharing a bottle of wine.

"Well?" Jessie asked, with an expectant look on her face.

"He bought it," he said, and chuckled. "But he wants me out of Serenity Quays immediately."

"Thank God I've almost finished packing," Sue said.

Jessie looked surprised. "Have you really?"

"Yes. We move into our new home at Lennox Head in two weeks," Sue replied.

The trio broke into laughter—their final bluff had paid off.

Chapter Twenty-One

"Arty, there's a little something I'd like you to do for me." It appeared to Bullpit that Dermot Bollinger had regained his composure after the previous day's fiasco. He had heard about Bollinger's amazing back-down over the motion that had been passed at the Tenants' Committee meeting, but Bullpit was wise enough not to mention the matter.

"Yes, sir. How can I help?" Bullpit replied.

His subservient manner pleased Bollinger. "This Curry arse hole, Arty, what do you know about him?" he asked.

"Not a lot, Mr. Bollinger. He's been at Serenity Quays for about two years, runs some sort of consulting business with his wife. He's a mate of Tony Bloom and the Major—they all play golf together. We checked him out last year when he ran for the Tenants' Committee." Bullpit chuckled. "We couldn't find any dirt on him, so we had to invent some."

"Well, you're going to be busy over the next week or so, Arty, because I want you to follow him around and check out what he's up to. With discretion, of course. This is highly confidential, so don't let him see you. I want to know how he got hold of the information about the sale."

"Leave him to me, sir," Bullpit said.

"There's one other matter that I'd like you to sort out for me, Arty."

"Anything, Mr. Bollinger, whatever I can do." Bullpit was enjoying himself—it was like the old days.

"There's a couple who have become a nuisance around Serenity Quays, and I want you to persuade them to get lost."

"I can handle any of the residents in Serenity Quays, Mr. Bollinger."

Bollinger grunted loudly. "This couple aren't residents, but they want to be, and they won't take no for an answer."

"I'll sort them out, Mr. Bollinger. What's their name?"

"They're a pair of old fogies by the name of Hawke. I have their address here somewhere in my diary."

"Do you want me to get rough with them, Mr. Bollinger?" Bullpit asked, after Bollinger had given him the address.

"Do whatever it takes, Arty. I'll leave it to you."

"I'll get on it right away, Mr. Bollinger. Usual retainer and expenses, sir?"

"Yes, Arty, the usual arrangement."

* * *

Gerry Curry had completed the photographic work he needed for the Davenport presentation, and had begun packing up his camera equipment. He'd made his way into the bushland behind Serenity Quays on foot, as vehicular traffic, even in a four-wheel drive, was impossible. Gerry had never ventured into this part of the resort before, because it was regarded as out of bounds for the residents. Gerry was delighted with what he saw. His flippant suggestion for the inclusion of a golf course was intended purely as a means of maintaining Joshua Davenport's interest in his services. Now he could see that a golf course would greatly add to the market potential of the new estate. From his observations, the nine-hole golfing facility he had recommended would be relatively inexpensive to construct, the contour of the land creating a natural layout for a golf course.

Gerry was taking in the view when he became aware of a noise—it was the sound of heavy machinery coming from further up the hillside. He moved towards the sound, picking his way through the heavy bush to a ridge overlooking two creeks that ran down to the river at the northern end of the resort. In the distance,

Gerry could make out a bobcat removing soil from a large mound near one of the creeks. When he moved closer, he could see that the operator was closing off a breach in one of the creeks. As Gerry watched, he realised that the break in the creek bank could not have occurred naturally. Someone had sabotaged the waterway, and the person in the bobcat below him was repairing the damage.

Gerry leant back against the rock wall. Could this be some of Bollinger's dirty work? Yes, he thought, with Dermot Bollinger, anything was bloody possible.

Gerry took his camera from its case and moved a little closer—he needed photographic evidence.

* * *

Arty Bullpit sat on the bank of the canal a short distance from Curry's house. Bullpit was fishing, a cover he thought to be quite ingenious. He watched as Curry moved off in the direction of heavy bushland on the western side of the resort. This was rough country, overrun with thick undergrowth on a steep, rocky hillside. Nobody ventured into that part of the estate because of the terrain. Then Bullpit noticed the carry bag over Curry's shoulder, and realised it was a camera case.

"Where the fuck are you going?" he mumbled to himself, as he moved off after him.

Bullpit had gone a short distance up the hillside when he stopped, gasping for breath—the climb was steeper than he had anticipated. He looked off in the distance and saw that Curry was almost out of sight. He took a deep breath and moved off after his disappearing prey. He had gone only a few paces when a rock he stepped on gave way and he half fell, half stumbled back down the hill from where he had started.

Bullpit sat on a rock ledge and held his badly skinned knee, cursing Curry for the pain and indignity he was suffering. "Why would anyone in their right mind want to take photos of this God forsaken place?" he said aloud. To Bullpit, following Curry up a dangerous mountain while he took photos of the wildlife seemed an absolute waste of time. But Arty Bullpit knew there was another reason why he was reluctant to follow Curry up the hillside. His terrifying experience on the recent bus trip with the Arab kid had left him with a disturbing fear of heights.

As Bullpit made his way out of the bush, he decided there was a far more interesting project to deal with, and it was a nice day for a drive to Lismore. He would pay a visit to Mr. and Mrs. Hawke.

As Bullpit drove through the security gates, he noticed Bollinger's car parked outside Grimes' office. He decided he would call in and discuss the strange mountain climbing exploits of Gerry Curry with his boss. Bullpit parked beside Bollinger's vehicle, and he was about to alight from his car when he hesitated. What if Bollinger insisted that he climb back up the hillside to see exactly what Curry was doing up there? No, he decided, he had done enough rock climbing for the day. He closed his car door and drove out of the resort in the direction of Lismore.

* * *

The Hawkes lived in a rundown house on a small farm just north of the town. The body of an abandoned sedan lay in the front yard and, amongst the weeds, pieces of rusty machinery and old motorbike parts were scattered everywhere. A large wooden shed stood at the rear of the house, with several Harley Davidson motorcycles parked out the front. Bullpit was studying the layout of the place when he was startled by a voice behind him.

"Lookin' for someone, mate?"

Bullpit turned, and when he saw the woman, he was unable to stifle a laugh. Minty Hawke was wearing her usual leather outfit, but her hairstyle had changed. It was now spiked and bright purple in colour.

"Christ, it's Cindy Lowper's grandmother," Bullpit said sarcastically.

"A comedian are we?" the woman said, with a hint of malice in her voice. "Would you mind telling me what you want, funny man?"

"Are you Mrs. Hawke?"

"Yes I am, sport, and who the fuck are you?"

Bullpit decided to adopt a more formal role. "I'm a representative from Serenity Quays, and I'm here to inform you and your husband that there's no place for you in our resort."

Minty Hawke slowly circled around Bullpit—like a wild cat moving in on its kill. "Is that so? And what, exactly, is your role at Serenity Quays, Mr. Representative?"

Bullpit was becoming annoyed with the woman's strange behaviour. "I'm...I'm the senior security officer, and I'm here to make sure you understand the owner's decision. You must stay away from our resort in the future."

"Well kiss my fanny," Minty said, and chuckled, "A geriatric standover man." She turned to the shed. "Morgan, get your fat arse out here," she yelled.

"We're in the middle of our bloody meeting," a voice called back from inside the shed.

"I need you out here now, you dumb arse prick—and bring the boys with you," she called back without taking her gaze off Bullpit.

The old wooden doors of the shed opened, and Morgan Hawke stepped out into the sunlight, followed by at least twenty members of the *Bikies from Hell* motorcycle club.

"This is Mr. Representative, from Serenity Quays. He's come here to kick our arse," Minty said, with a menacing look in her eyes.

* * *

An uneasy peace existed between Felicity Grimes and her boss, and so it would remain—their relationship would never be the same. After recent events, neither one really trusted the other.

"It seems everyone wants to choose their own block at Hideaway Cove." Bollinger was concerned by the likelihood of unrest amongst the residents of Serenity Quays. "Relocating the whingeing old bastards is going to be hell."

"Not really," Felicity replied, "We'll place each resident within their own category."

Bollinger raised his eyebrows. "Their what?" he asked.

Felicity smiled. "Every resident in Serenity Quays is categorised, Dermot. How do you think I manage to keep the peace around here?"

"Please explain," he asked in a sarcastic tone.

"Have you heard the expression, *Bollinger's mob*?" Felicity asked.

"Who are they?" he asked.

"It's your group, Dermot—the people loyal to you. Naylor, Scraggs, Bullpit, and the others who support management in everything we do—they're *Category 1*."

My own mob of loyal supporters, Bollinger thought, and he flushed with pride.

"*Category 2* residents are also supportive, not as close, but friendly with Bollinger's mob because they're drinking mates at the sports club."

Bollinger nodded and Felicity continued.

Most residents are middle of the road, and they're *Category 3,* but they need to be watched. Take Sissy Witherspoon, for instance. She used to be a *Category 3* until she went over to the other side."

"The other side?" Bollinger asked.

"Yes, they're the *Category 4's,* the troublemakers. You've met them all over the past few days—Bloom, Curry, the Major, and their wives. Controllable most of the time, but unpredictable. That group can be dangerous, as we've seen recently."

Bollinger looked at Grimes with admiration. And to think a few days ago he was going to ship her off to Tasmania. "So you'll place every one of similar persuasion together on the estate?"

Felicity nodded. "Exactly. Just as we sit them together at our dances on Saturday nights."

"And if anyone objects to their new neighbours?" he asked.

"Too bad. They go where I put them," Felicity replied confidently. In the past few days, Felicity Grimes had regained all her old fire.

"Well, you may need to make a few changes, Felicity. I've made commitments to several people."

Felicity eyed Bollinger suspiciously. "Commitments to whom?" she asked.

"Quinsy Naylor for one. He wants to be near the beach," he said, pointing to a building site on the large map spread out before them. "He's chosen Lot 89."

Felicity looked at the map, then back to Bollinger. "But that block is next to…"

Bollinger held up his hand. "If that's the site Quinsy wants, I think we should let him have it, don't you, Felicity?"

Felicity smiled. The cunning old bastard, what's he up too? she thought. "Definitely, Dermot, I think Quinsy *should* have lot 89, if that's what *he* wants—and the others?"

Bollinger pointed to an area at the top end of the resort. "I've promised Bullpit and Scraggs a site in this general area."

Felicity glared as she studied the map. "What a pity we can't have *The Three Stooges* close together," she said.

Bollinger laughed. "I'll leave it with you, Felicity. You'll know what to do," he said, getting to his feet. "I'm needed back on the Sunshine Coast."

* * *

Stanley Bancroft sat on his verandah, staring across the still waters of the canal. The sun was setting, and there was a golden haze shimmering on the water from the afternoon sky. A book of poems by Omar Khayyam lay discarded on the table beside him. Stanley was deeply distressed. The decision to close Serenity Quays had come as a shock for him, and his life was now in turmoil. The planned move to Hideaway Cove, and the uncertainties it had created, filled him with fear and apprehension.

What remained of his wonderful garden was now assembled in dozens of plastic pots around his property. It had taken him years to establish his garden, and to start again seemed impossible for him to even contemplate. He had been offered a block backing onto the magnificent lake at Hideaway Cove, and Benny and Maurice would still be his neighbours, but Stanley was very happy at Serenity Quays, and did not want to leave. Now, his sheltered and well-organised life was in disarray.

And what was to become of Mr. DeAngelo? It was almost a month since the last incident, and Stanley was unsure if the old man would be joining them at Hideaway Cove. Ricky had rung once to say that Roberto had been discharged from hospital into the care of his sister. He had fully recovered, Ricky said, apart from a rope burn scar on his neck and a raspy voice. Try as he may, it had been impossible for Stanley to put poor Mr. DeAngelo out of his mind.

A knock on his front door startled Stanley. He had fallen asleep in the patio chair, and now it was dark. Stanley was still not fully awake when he opened his front door. He stared for a moment at the old man standing in his doorway, dressed like he was going to someone's funeral.

"Mr. DeAngelo, you're back," was all he could manage to say.

"Yeah, I'm back," DeAngelo muttered, "and I wanna tell you I'm not gonna kill myself no more."

"That's wonderful, Mr. DeAngelo, I'm so pleased."

"I'm glad you pleased, Bancroft," DeAngelo replied in his raspy voice, "because I'm gonna kill you instead." DeAngelo then turned on his short bandy legs and, a little unsteadily, stormed off towards his own house.

Stanley stood on his front porch for some time after the old man had gone, trying to decide what he should do. Finally, he retreated inside the house and locked the door behind him. As he closed the blinds to his lounge room, Stanley peered out into the darkness, but Roberto was nowhere in sight. Then Stanley remembered the patio door; he had left it open when he answered the front door. As Stanley turned, he gasped loudly—he was too late. Watching him from the dining room was Ricky DeAngelo and his two goons. They had entered through his unlocked patio door. And standing in the doorway was the old man.

"Get rid of him," Roberto said, and shuffled off into the darkness.

Scarface rushed forward and grabbed Stanley by the shoulders. He held him firmly while the albino taped his arms and legs.

"We gotta make this look good, Bancroft," Ricky said. "If he finds out you're still alive, he's gonna come back and do the job himself."

"Why me?" Stanley asked in annoyance, as scarface forced him, bound tightly, into his favourite lounge chair.

"Because he hates you—and because his *shrink* told him to. It was, how you say, good therapy for him. It helped him get his mind off other things."

"The psychiatrist redirected his feelings of depression into a vendetta against me? That's outrageous!" Stanley cried as he struggled against his bondage.

"Yeah, Bancroft, maybe. But it worked, right? He ain't tried to kill himself no more."

"So, how long do you think it will take him to realise I'm still around? We *are* neighbours, you know."

"Not for long, Bancroft. We sold Poppa's house back to that *cane toad* who owns this dump. When you get back, Poppa ain't gonna be your neighbour no more."

"When I get back—where am I going?"

"On a little holiday for a few weeks, okay? Now, when Poppa comes in the room, after we shoot you, play dead. Don't move, don't breath, don't do nothin', just lay still on the floor. You gotta look dead, okay?"

Ricky nodded and the albino placed a strip of tape over Stanley's mouth.

Scarface removed a revolver from his coat pocket, then fixed an attachment to the muzzle. He pushed Stanley roughly to the floor and a moment later there were two dull thuds, then an acrid smell in the air.

"I gonna get Poppa now, Bancroft, so don't move. After we're gone, someone will get you outa here and take you some place safe you gonna like, okay?"

A few minutes later Stanley heard muffled voices, then silence for what seemed an eternity. After some time, there was movement in the room and he froze in fear. Had Poppa come back, he wondered, to make sure he had been properly *got rid of*?

As strong hands gently turned him on his side, Stanley looked up into the most beautiful dark brown eyes he had ever seen. "Who are you?" he asked, after the woman had removed the tape from his mouth.

"I'm your driver, Mr. Bancroft. Ricky sent me. I'm taking you to the Gold Coast." When she had removed the rest of the tape, she helped him to his feet. "Now," she said, looking around anxiously, "throw some clothes in a bag and we'll be on our way."

Fifteen minutes later they had left Serenity Quays and were heading north. "Where're we going?" Stanley asked.

"I'm taking you to my place at Burleigh Heads, Mr. Bancroft. It's right on the beach; I think you'll like it there."

Stanley studied the woman closely in the dim interior of the car—she was beautiful. "What's your name?" he asked.

"Angelica," she replied.

"Well, Angelica, if we're going to be travelling all that way together, you may as well call me Stanley."

She turned and smiled at him. It was a wonderful smile. "All right, Stanley," she said softly.

"Do you like poetry, Angelica?" he asked.

"Oh yes, Stanley, I love poetry, particularly the English poets, like Shelley and Robert Browning. They were such romantics."

They were quiet for a period with only the hum of the engine and the whirr of the tyres breaking the silence.

"Angelica," Stanley said, "how will your family feel about me coming to stay?"

When she turned to him, Stanley saw the sadness in her eyes. "I live alone, Stanley," she said. "I'm a widow. My husband died ten years ago."

Stanley sighed. "I find it very lonely being on my own, Angelica. Do you?" he asked.

"Yes I do, Stanley, very lonely." She smiled at him again. "So I'm going to enjoy your company for the next three weeks."

As Stanley settled back, watching the blackness rushing by his window, he felt a poem tumbling through his mind. A poem about an angel, with soft olive skin, ebony hair as black as midnight, and the largest brown eyes he had ever seen. It was a poem about the mysteries of lovemaking, soon to be unfurled by a beautiful woman—the woman of his dreams.

Chapter Twenty-Two

"This will be our last get-together," Quinsy Naylor said to the group gathered around in the sports club for their final drinking session. The clubrooms were about to be demolished, and within a week, most of them would be moving to their new homes in Hideaway Cove. "It's going to be a long time before we can meet like this again," Quinsy said. "There was no money left for our sports club after that stupid motion was passed."

"Well, I'm glad we got the motion passed," Hank Van Hooganband replied. "Bugger the sports club."

There was a low rumble of agreement from the group that had settled in for an afternoon of serious drinking.

"As president of the sports club, and speaking on behalf of the members, I would like to welcome back our old mate, Moose Dart," Quinsy announced.

"What's it like in Her Majesty's Federal Prison, Moose?" Marty Fisk asked, as he opened a can of beer. Marty's wife Jo Jo had banned him from making another batch of home brew.

"Get stuffed," Moose replied, glaring angrily at Marty. Moose had been strangely quiet since he spent three weeks in jail, which culminated in a charge of illegally selling prescription drugs.

"When you're back in the Viagra business, Moose, let me know, I'm running down—if you know what I mean," Willy Hogan said, causing everyone to break out into raucous laughter.

"Anyone who wants to go and see Arty Bullpit can visit him in hospital next week," Quinsy sadly informed the group. "He came out of intensive care yesterday, but only two visitors at a time are allowed."

"How's he doing?" Willy Hogan asked.

"Not so good," Quinsy replied in a mournful tone. "He'll be in hospital for another three weeks, then on crutches for at least three months, the Doc says."

"What was he trying to prove, picking a fight with twenty bikies?" Gill Trotter asked.

"No one seems to know. All he keeps mumbling is that some bikies' mole, with purple hair, wouldn't stop kicking him in the nuts," Quinsy explained.

"Poor old Arty," Willy Hogan said in a sympathetic voice. "Him stuck in hospital, and all of us off to the Tweed Coast."

The group raised their glasses. "To Arty Bullpit," they toasted.

* * *

At the same time, a short distance away, the Major and his wife, the Blooms, and the Currys were having their final drink together on Gerry's verandah. Sue and Gerry were moving to their new house at Lennox Head in a few days.

"Bollinger can't wait to get rid of us," Sue said. "He wants to settle first thing on Friday."

"Well, we don't want you to go," Evy replied.

"You're not getting rid of us that easily. We'll only be an hour's drive away," Sue said.

"Are you going to tell us what you've been up to for the past four weeks, Gerry?" the Major asked.

"Don't worry, Major, all will be revealed in due time," Gerry replied.

"Here's to the good fight, and may it continue at Hideaway Cove," Tony Bloom said, with a touch of sadness in his voice.

"To the good fight," everyone toasted.

* * *

170

The following morning, Tony and Evy Bloom were busy packing when they received a phone call. Tony looked at Evy and shrugged when the caller identified herself.

"We need to talk, Tony." It was Felicity Grimes.

"Yes, Felicity," he answered abruptly.

"Not over the phone, and certainly not in my office," she said. "Somewhere outside of Serenity Quays, if we can."

"What about the coffee shop at the pier?" he said, a little more politely. "In about half an hour?"

"I'll see you there," she said.

"Well I'll be buggered," he said to Evy, as he hung up the phone. "The enemy wants to talk."

Tony was surprised by the unexpected phone call, and as he drove into town, he wondered what Felicity Grimes was up to. After eight years of conflict, he was surprised by her conciliatory manner on the phone. Caution was needed, he decided. He had been a victim of Felicity's devious actions before.

"I think it's time your group and I got together," Felicity said after they had ordered their coffee.

"Why the sudden change, Felicity? You've given us hell since we moved into Serenity Quays."

"I'm sorry, Tony, I was just doing my job—doing what Bollinger told me to do."

Tony studied the woman closely—he wanted to believe her. "Why, Felicity? You're going to be the new resident manager at Hideaway Cove. Why the change?"

Felicity opened a satchel of sugar and poured it into her coffee. "I don't want Scraggs to be involved in the running of Hideaway Cove," she said.

"Why?" Tony asked.

"Because he's on Bollinger's payroll."

"You're kidding?"

"I'm not. Apparently he's been Bollinger's mole for the past eight years. He's even been spying on me."

"Jesus," Tony said, as he sat back and took a sip of his coffee. "But why are you worried that he'll have anything to do with running the resort? There's no way he'd get elected to a committee. Most of the residents hate his guts."

"Bollinger has a plan, Tony." She hesitated. "Have you noticed who's being moved into Hideaway Cove first?"

Tony considered the question. "Yes, all Bollinger's lot, his *Category 1* and *2* pals...so?"

"Bollinger, Scraggs, and Bullpit had a meeting at my house last week. They plan to call a Tenants' Committee meeting of *Category 1* and *2* residents when they have the numbers on site at Hideaway Cove. They'll elect a new committee there, with Scraggs as chairman and Naylor as secretary."

Tony looked annoyed. "They can't do that."

"Yes they can, Tony. Bollinger's checked it out. There's no provision in your constitution to cover this situation. You have to call an emergency meeting before we start moving people next week. You must amend the constitution to ensure your existing committee can continue to represent the tenants when we all move to Hideaway Cove."

Tony leant forward. "Why are you sticking your neck out like this, Felicity?"

"After eight years, I'm sick of the fighting. Now I want what's best for the tenants of Hideaway Cove." She smiled. "I think you and Sissy will be fantastic for the resort."

* * *

The following day, a special meeting was held to vote on an important amendment to the constitution, regarding the carry-over of recently elected office bearers at Serenity Quays to Hideaway Cove. A ninety percent majority carried the amendment, which, Quinsy Naylor admitted, was a massive snub by his friends from the sports club.

* * *

Moose Dart was a forlorn looking figure as he sat in Dolly Mott's lounge room, bemoaning his shattered distribution business. His last consignment of Cialis lay hidden under Dolly's bed, and he had no way of disposing of it—not without risking another confrontation with the Federal Police. If he was found selling prescription drugs to his friends again, he would go to jail for at least a year, the magistrate had told him. But Moose was determined to get his money back. He had most of his savings tied up in the shipment, and there was a ready-made market out there for the product.

Moose watched Dolly as she iced her lamingtons, then tossed them in shredded coconut. Dolly Mott's lamingtons were renowned in Serenity Quays, and were always the first cakes to go at any function, or stall, where they were sold. Dolly made a cup of tea for them both, placed one of the lamingtons on a plate, and handed it to Moose.

"Here," she said. "This might cheer you up."

"The only thing that'll cheer me up is findin' a way to sell that stock without getting caught," he mumbled.

As he bit into the fresh sponge cake, his hands became covered in chocolate icing and coconut pieces. He placed the lamington on the plate and began licking his fingers. "Maybe," he said between licks, "we could mix them in with your lamingtons."

173

He gave his fingers a final lick, and laughed. "Dolly's aphrodisiac lamingtons."

Moose picked up the lamington again, and with the cake halfway to his mouth, he stopped and looked at Dolly.

"What?" she said.

There was a look of excitement on Moose's face. "Why *don't* we mix the tablets in with your lamingtons?"

Dolly's eyes lit up, and she grinned. "Moose, you're a genius," she said.

"I can crush the tablets down to a powder, then we'll mix one into each lamington." Moose held up a chocolate covered finger. "We'll sell them for five dollars each."

"Or three for ten dollars," Dolly added.

Moose got to his feet and began pacing the floor. "This is a brilliant cover, Dolly. Only our customers will know what we're selling," he said.

Dolly was thoughtful for a moment. "What about the taste? Will that be a problem?" she asked.

"Dunno. Let's make some and see," he said excitedly.

"Why don't we sell them as *herbal* lamingtons? That way we can explain away any queries about the flavour," Dolly suggested.

Moose pointed a supportive finger at Dolly. "Yeah, we'll just say that it's the herbs and spices they can taste."

"I've even got a slogan," Dolly said. "Now you *can* have your cake and eat it too."

Moose laughed heartily. "Or, no more nasty tablets, now they come as a Devonshire Tea."

Dolly sighed, and there was wistful look on her face. "Dolly's herbal lamingtons," she said.

* * *

A few days later, Moose and one of his regular customers, Silvio Ottoman, stood on Moose's verandah haggling over the price. "Five bucks each is a bit steep, Moose. We're pensioners, you know."

"Well, take three for ten dollars then," Moose replied. "Remember, Silvio, Dolly's lamington is included in the price."

"I don't like lamingtons," Silvio said, and screwed up his face.

Moose was becoming frustrated. "They're not normal lamingtons, Silvio, they're—you know—special."

"Okay, but if I don't like them, can I bring them back?"

"Sorry Silvio, no refunds. They might have gone stale."

Begrudgingly, Silvio Ottoman took his three lamingtons. "Okay, I'll take them, Moose, but at that price the bloody things had better work."

The following afternoon, Silvio Ottoman was back knocking on Moose Dart's front door.

"I told you, Silvio, no returns," Moose said, as he went to close his door.

"I don't have any returns," Silvio said. "I want three more."

Moose looked at the man closely and cocked his head. "Hey, Silvio, how many of those things did you eat?" he asked, a little concerned.

"None. My wife took them to the Ladies Auxiliary meeting at the church this morning."

"She did what?"

"The ladies loved them. So did Monsignor Hopgood. In fact, the Monsignor wants to know if he can put a weekly order in for a dozen of Dolly's herbal Lamingtons."

* * *

Felicity Grimes was relieved when her caller identified himself. "Mr. Bancroft, we've been worried about you. Where've you been?"

There was silence for a moment before Stanley answered. "Didn't you get my note saying I'd be away for awhile?"

"Yes I did, but that was three weeks ago. We're beginning to move everyone into Hideaway Cove, and you haven't signed your new lease agreement yet."

There was another short silence before Stanley replied. "I'm afraid I won't be joining you at Hideaway Cove, Felicity. I'm moving overseas, so I'll be accepting Mr. Bollinger's offer to buy my house."

Felicity was confused. This *was* Stanley Bancroft with whom she was speaking. The Stanley Bancroft who hardly went beyond his flower garden during the eight years he lived at Serenity Quays.

"Overseas—where overseas?" she asked.

"To Florence. That's where I'm phoning from now," Stanley replied.

"Florence, Italy?" Felicity stammered.

"Yes, Felicity, and tomorrow I'm getting married."

"Stanley Bancroft, getting married, that's wonderful, Stanley. Who...where did you meet...?"

Stanley interrupted her stammering response. "It's a long story, Felicity, but I'm marrying a beautiful lady—her name's Angelica."

Felicity was so overcome with the news that she began to cry. Stanley Bancroft was one tenant she really liked. "I'm so pleased for you, Stanley, and I hope you'll be very happy." She wiped her eyes and took a deep breath. "Now, is there anything you want done at the house?"

"There's a few things you could do for me, Felicity. The removalists will be coming to pack and move my belongings in the next few days, so they'll need a key. And would you give all my plants to Benny and Maurice. The boys always admired my garden. One other thing I must ask of you, Felicity, which may sound a little strange. If you see Mr. DeAngelo, don't mention to him that you were talking with me—under any circumstances."

Felicity hesitated. "I won't be seeing Mr. DeAngelo, Stanley. I'm afraid he's dead. His son Ricky rang me yesterday. It appears his father wanted to return to work in the family business. They found him sitting slumped at his desk on his first day back at work. He'd apparently died from a heart attack."

Felicity listened, but there was no response from Stanley. Then, just before the line went dead, she thought she heard him crying.

* * *

Brendan O'Brien leant back on his stool and sipped his glass of iced tea. The large sliding doors of the hotel bar were pushed fully open, allowing access to the soft tropical breezes, while the Coral Sea could be heard lapping the sand on the beach just a short distance away.

"Palm Cove is magnificent," O'Brien said, and sighed deeply. "This must be the Paradise I was always preaching about."

The woman on the stool next him turned and smiled. "So you're a preacher then?" she asked.

O'Brien scratched the five-day stubble on his chin and rubbed the hairs on his tanned chest through his partly opened tropical shirt. "Until four weeks ago I was a priest, but I fell into temptation, and had to give it away."

"Oh really, what sort of temptation?" the woman asked.

"I was having lustful visions of one of my female parishioners. I kept seeing her, lying naked, on the front pew of my church while I was giving my Sunday sermon."

The woman looked at him and smiled. "So you gave up the priesthood because of the images you had of this woman. I think that's rather romantic."

O'Brien shrugged and sipped his drink. "And what about you? What brings you to North Queensland?"

"Oh, I've had my problems too. I fell in love with a married man, and it caused my own marriage to fall apart. I left, and came up here to start a new life."

"This married man, do you still love him?" O'Brien asked.

"Well, it seems he's no longer married, and yes, I still love him."

"Have you told him?" he asked.

"Yes, I told him in confession once, when he was still a priest, and married to the Church."

O'Brien scratched his chin again. "I need a deck hand. Do you know anything about boats?"

"Never been on a boat in my life," she replied.

"Good," he said, and grinned. " I'll teach you."

He took her hand and led her from the bar. At the entrance, she stopped and looked up at him. "By the way, do I have to lie around naked on this boat of yours?"

"Absolutely!" O'Brien replied.

She hesitated for a moment. "Sounds like fun," she said, and laughed. Agnes Hoskiss placed her arms around his waist and kissed him on the cheek. "Now, let me see this boat of yours."

Chapter Twenty-Three

It was a full house at Aussie Stadium, and the giant arena was charged with great excitement. There were over seventy thousand rugby fans on hand to see Australia try and win back the Bledisloe Cup from the Kiwis. The lights dimmed, and a spotlight was thrown onto an elevated stage in the centre of the ground. Then a voice thundered across the stadium: "Ladies and gentlemen, please be upstanding for the Australian National Anthem."

The military band burst into life with their introduction of *Advance Australia Fair*. Then, a magnificent tenor voice began a rendition of the anthem unlike anything that had been heard before. The extraordinary voice filled every corner of the stadium with such clarity and resonance that people wept from the sheer exhilaration of the sound. With his last lyrical chord, the stadium fell silent, as if stunned by the performance. Dizzy Abood stood back from the microphone and bowed his head slightly. Then, seconds later, the stadium erupted in a tumultuous roar.

From his position on the centre stage, Dizzy looked to a position high above the main arena and waved a salute to Penny Applebee and his mother, the two women happily embracing each other as the stadium crowd continued to applaud the brilliant young singer making his first public appearance.

* * *

Muriel and Quinsy Naylor stood watching the landscape gardeners put the finishing touches to the small area of land around their new home at Hideaway Cove. Things had gone badly for Quinsy since he was dumped from the Tenants' Committee. Dermot Bollinger and Felicity Grimes now avoided him, and some of his drinking mates were ignoring him too. Even his old friend

Bullpit was a little curt when he last visited him in hospital. His feeling of isolation had worsened, because there was no longer a sports club where he could escape to and go drinking with the boys. But the thing that was causing Quinsy the most distress was the location of their new house.

"I thought you said it was the block nearest to the beach?" Muriel asked, glaring at him angrily.

Quinsy looked nervous and hunched his shoulders. "Well, according to the plan, we *are* closest to the beach."

Muriel turned and looked to an area just beyond their house, where a three-metre wire fence extended around the eastern perimeter of the resort. Beyond the fence, a large sand dune concealed a busy roadway, and the beach a short distance away.

"How do you expect me to get to the beach from here—climb over a bloody great fence?" she said, pointing towards the unsightly obstruction. "And why are we stuck down here at the end of the resort? We can't see the lake, we're miles from the pool and bowling-green, and nowhere near any of my friends." It was all too much for Muriel and she burst into tears.

Quinsy knew it would be impossible to console her. He never could when she got into one of these moods. And there was little Quinsy could say, anyway. She was right; he had chosen the very worst block in the resort. But how was he to know there was no access to the beach from the block he chose? There was no fence on the plan Bollinger had shown him. And why were Bullpit and Scraggs on the other side of the resort, near the pool and the recreational buildings? Quinsy shook his head in dismay. If he didn't know better, he could almost imagine that this situation had been deliberately planned.

* * *

Dwayne Gannet sat impatiently in his truck, waiting to begin his work. Bollinger had demanded his immediate presence at

Serenity Quays because he needed some demolition work done. As he waited, his anger grew. He was a qualified civil engineer, not a house demolisher—but what could he do? Bollinger hadn't paid him for his work on the creek wall, and there was the photographic evidence he was holding over him.

Having left Brisbane before sun-up, Gannet now realised that his work on the house could not start until much later in the day. The furniture removalist would need at least two hours to load the old man's possessions, and there would be a further delay while the tradesmen disconnected the water and power. To add to their problems, Felicity Grimes and the man's daughter were having trouble getting him to leave the house.

Gannet laughed when he heard the owner yelling at the two women. The old man had seen the removalist van and guessed something sinister was being planned. Now he refused to budge from his home.

Gannet climbed down from his truck and made his way towards the house. He had waited long enough, he told himself. If the women couldn't persuade him to leave, he would remove the old man physically—then everyone could get on with their work.

Gannet was about to knock on the front door when it was flung open, and the old man stood in the doorway, scowling at him. Behind him the two women were in close pursuit. He pushed open the screen door and grabbed Gannet by the arms. "Where've you been?" the old man shouted. "I called the agency days ago."

"What are you talking about?" Gannet asked, totally confused by the man's question.

"You're the special agent that's going to eliminate these two, aren't you?" he asked, jerking his thumb at the two women, who now had a firm hold of him.

Gannet laughed. It was a vicious, cruel laugh that made the man's daughter gasp. "Get your hands off me, you stupid old fool," he said, with all the vitriol he could summon. "I'm here to demolish your bloody house."

There was a bewildered look on the old man's face, and his knees buckled beneath him. The two women took his weight and began moving him towards a car that was parked nearby.

The daughter glared at Gannet as they passed, and there was hatred in her eyes. "You bastard!" she said, through clenched teeth.

As they reached the car, the man began to struggle violently. He looked back at Gannet, and there were tears in his eyes. "Please don't hurt my friends," he pleaded.

A moment later the car was gone.

* * *

The demolition job took Gannet less than two hours, plus another thirty minutes to load the unwanted building onto the back of his truck. What was once the old man's home was now a pile of rubble about to be dumped at the local tip.

The sun was setting as Gannet squatted beside the lake with his back to the now vacant block of land. As he looked out over the still waters of the holding lake, he began to take stock of his current situation. He could send Bollinger a copy of the original quotation with a letter of demand for the seven grand that he was refusing to pay. But what good would that do? Bollinger would ignore the demand, unless he took the matter to court—but if he took court action, Bollinger would release the incriminating photographs to the authorities. Dwayne Gannet suddenly realised that he had become trapped in Bollinger's evil clutches.

An old plastic bucket lay on the ground near Gannet's feet. "One day, Bollinger, one day..." he shouted, and kicked the bucket out into the lake.

As Gannet headed back towards his truck, two large green eyes appeared from beneath the water of the lake, and watched him as he drove away.

* * *

The last of Stanley's furniture was being loaded into the van, and Felicity was checking through a pile of rubbish lying in the middle of the floor of his empty lounge room. She had promised Stanley that she would do a final inspection before the removalist departed. Felicity was satisfied with the work until she noticed a cushion lying amongst the rubbish.

"What's that?" she asked the foreman, pointing to the discarded cushion.

"Didn't think it was worth packing, lady, with two bloody holes in it."

As the removalists drove away, Felicity stood in the doorway remembering a time eight years earlier when she had shown a reluctant Stanley Bancroft around the house. She recalled how it had taken all her marketing skills and persuasive powers to get him to put down a deposit and sign the lease.

They were tough times, she recalled—struggling to establish the resort, and to sell the first few homes—but she remembered them fondly. Over the past few weeks she had begun to realise how much she loved Serenity Quays—the resort was part of her. Soon it would be over, and she knew Hideaway Cove would not be the same. Despite the daily grind of maintaining its peaceful environment, she really enjoyed her time at Serenity Quays, and now she didn't want it to end—certainly not destroyed like this.

As she stood reminiscing about the past, hugging Stanley's discarded cushion, she noticed a strange, acrid smell emanating from the two ragged holes. As she turned the cushion over, something fell to the floor beside her feet. She bent down and picked up two pieces of jagged metal. She turned them over in her hand, and was confused. What had come from inside the cushion appeared to be two misshapen bullets.

* * *

Lily Hartmann had made her decision—she would return to Israel. Since the loss of her dear husband, and her much loved parrot, Lily had been very distressed. While there had been a marked improvement in her mental state since the *incident* involving her neighbour's exploding home brew, Lily now had a reason to return to her native homeland.

Lily had a science degree from the University of Tel Aviv, and had worked for her Country's security services for many years before coming to Australia with her husband. Now Lily was returning home to take up a technical position in a highly secretive division of the Israeli military, in her field of expertise.

"We're going to miss you, Lily," Felicity Grimes said, as they finalised the sale of her house. "What do you plan to do when you get back to Israel?"

"I'm going into the secret…" she paused. "I'm going to rejoin the army."

Felicity looked up from the paperwork she was preparing and stared at the woman sitting opposite her. "The army—you're joining the army?" she repeated, struggling to restrain herself from laughing. "What would *you* do in the army, Lily?"

Lily felt pressured by the question. Secrecy was the hallmark of her operational unit, and a crucial part of her specialised training. "I do… what you say here—specialised work."

"Oh, how exciting," Felicity replied, returning to her paperwork. Silly old bitch is losing it, she thought. Obviously, the death of her cocky had a more serious effect on her mental state than people realised.

Lily smiled to herself, sensing what Felicity was thinking. She found it hard to believe herself. At fifty-nine, Sergeant Lily Hartmann, operative 2098411 of the special bomb squad, was returning to her post as a field instructor, specialising in the use and detection of hi tech plastic explosives and detonating devices.

* * *

The Major stood on the elevated tee and looked down the fairway towards the green. It was Sunday morning, and this would be his last visit to their magnificent par three golf hole. To the Major, the fairway looked to be in pristine condition—probably better than he had ever seen it. Even though Hideaway Cove had its own nine-hole golf course, he knew somehow that it would never be the same as this. Now things were about to change. In two days time, he and Jessie would move to Hideaway Cove, and he would probably join one of the golf clubs in the area. Tony and Evy had already moved, and Gerry and Sue had settled into their new home at Lennox Head.

He recalled the many hours of hard work it had taken his friends and him and to establish and maintain the course the way they wanted it. But it was pleasant work, made even more enjoyable by the friendships that had been forged as they toiled together to achieve their common goal. Over the years, the game of golf the Major came to enjoy most of all was his Sunday morning practice sessions with his friends. Sadly, the Major realised, *that* time was gone forever.

"You're going to miss this aren't you?" a voice behind him said softly.

The Major turned to see Felicity Grimes looking down the fairway. "More than you can imagine," he replied, unable to hide the sadness he was feeling.

"I think I do know," she said. "I've grown to love this place too."

The Major looked at the woman by his side, and there were tears in her eyes. The Major was surprised. Felicity had been a tough adversary in the past, and he had never seen her show very much emotion. "I always thought you hated this place," he said.

Felicity smiled. "I hated you sometimes, when you were nasty to me," she said. "But I never hated Serenity Quays."

"Was I really that hard on you, Felicity, that you hated me?"

She shrugged. "Probably not, but we did have some super stoushes, didn't we, Major?"

The Major smiled. "We sure did, Felicity." He turned towards her. "I wonder if they'll continue—after we get to Hideaway Cove?"

Felicity giggled. "I hope so, Major, I certainly hope so."

Jessie was making her way towards the tee when she stopped and stood staring in disbelief. In front of her, not ten paces away, were Serenity Quays' two archenemies, her husband and Felicity Grimes. They were standing together, their arms around each other's waists, looking out across the Major's beloved golf course, and to the magnificent waterways of Serenity Quays beyond.

Chapter Twenty-Four

Dermot Bollinger wandered down to the small sandy beach where the land jutted out into the main holding lake. Bollinger loved this particular block. Even before the first house was built on the estate, he would stand on the very same spot and imagine what Serenity Quays would look like when it was finished. Now the block was vacant again, cleared several weeks earlier by Dwayne Gannet. Bollinger tried to recall the name of the old guy who had lived on the site for the past eight years, but he couldn't remember.

Bollinger sat down on the nearby pontoon, rolled up his trousers, and removed his sneakers. It was late afternoon and the humidity was stifling. A cyclone had been reported moving into the Tasman Sea, and the coastal air was oppressive and still. He placed his feet in the cool waters of the lake, leant back on his hands, and closed his eyes to the sun's glare.

Bollinger was feeling very pleased with himself. All but twenty houses had been removed from the site, and within three weeks, those, too, would be broken down into two sections and moved to his residential parks at Noosaville, Hideaway Cove, or his new resort at Port Macquarie. His team was well ahead of schedule, shipping out an average of seven homes a week, thanks to *his* organisational skills.

Not everything had gone the way Bollinger had planned in the past few months. His team had lost control of the Tenants' Committee at Hideaway Cove, and he was forced to enter into some unprofitable arrangements with the outgoing tenants at Serenity Quays. But despite these setbacks, Bollinger was still elated with the outcome—the sale of the resort would produce a huge windfall for his company.

Gaining ownership of the Serenity Quays site had been a lucky break for Bollinger. He had loaned a business friend two hundred thousand dollars to develop the project ten years earlier. By the time the site had been drained, the canal system created, and the roadways and other infrastructure completed, budget overruns had left the developer in financial difficulties.

That was when Bollinger made his move. He demanded payment of his loan immediately, or he would take legal action, a move that would force his friend into liquidation. The developer had no choice. Scraggs had masterminded a surreptitious clause in the contract, ensuring that the development site would revert to Bollinger in the event of non-payment of the loan. The memory of that transaction had always brought a great deal of pleasure to Bollinger, and he smiled as he recalled his cunning business propensity. On his latest reckoning, he stood to net more than twenty-one million dollars profit from the sale of Serenity Quays.

After almost forty years in business, Bollinger had achieved the level of wealth that he had sought all his life. But more importantly, he now had the financial resources to develop his most ambitious project yet, the jewel in the crown—Bella Vista Mews, on Sydney's Northern Beaches. He was able to negotiate a one hundred-year lease on the land, and now he would build seventy-five of his best homes on the site. The profit margins would be enormous, he told himself—as much as three hundred thousand per house, and rentals of twenty thousand a year. If he could get twenty-two million for Serenity Quays, he could get five times that much for Bella Vista. Bollinger was so overcome with the prospect of such unimagined wealth that his whole body trembled with delight.

And there was one other reward that would come from the capital gain he would make on Serenity Quays. He had been offered a quarter share in a *Lear Jet*, the ultimate status symbol for any Queensland property developer. No more commercial airline flights or long trips in his car—now he could visit each of his five resorts in his own jet aircraft. Bollinger flushed with a deep sense of personal adulation as he sat contemplating his achievements, and he was filled with overwhelming euphoria.

Bollinger was so preoccupied in his self-indulgence that he failed to notice a movement in the bushes not far from where he was sitting. Then, near a grassy embankment, where the lake joined the first canal, something plunged into the water with a loud splash, then disappeared under the surface. Bollinger studied the area for a moment, watching the water for any further movement. Then his mobile phone rang.

"Bollinger speaking," he said, not taking his eyes from the point in the lake where the disturbance had occurred.

Beneath the surface something large moved in his direction.

"Mr. Bollinger, this is Mark Munro. I'm the chief engineer with the Council."

"I know who you are, Mr. Munro. What can I do for you?" he replied, his eyes still focussed on the lake.

"We have a problem at Serenity Quays, Mr. Bollinger, a very serious problem that we need to discuss with you."

Bollinger tuned his attention to the caller. "Problem, what sort of problem?" There was an anxious tone in his voice.

"We've received some disturbing evidence from a member of the public." The engineer hesitated. "It's a claim that someone has been interfering with the water courses above Serenity Quays."

Bollinger sat stunned for a moment, then swung his legs out of the water. He got to his feet just as the unseen menace reached the pontoon. Bollinger was so preoccupied with the conversation that he failed to notice a wild splash of water as *the thing* turned sharply away from where, a moment earlier, he had been sitting.

"What sort of evidence?" Bollinger asked in an abrupt manner.

"Photographs and a statuary declaration…"

189

"Photographs?" Bollinger interrupted. "Photographs of what?"

"Photographs of a bobcat operator breaching the wall of one of the creeks," the engineer replied. "The CEO was wondering if we could arrange a suitable time for you to come into our office and discuss the matter with us."

Gannet, Bollinger thought immediately. The bastard's taken his own photographs, then gone to the authorities with his version of the events. Bollinger rolled down the legs of his slacks and slipped on his sneakers. "I'm on the Sunshine Coast at the moment," Bollinger lied. There was no way he was meeting with Council without his solicitor being present. "Could you fax or e-mail me the details?" he asked, as he hurried towards his car parked in front of the vacant block.

The engineer hesitated, uncertain if he should press the issue. Bollinger's secretary had earlier advised him that her boss was in the area, inspecting the Serenity Quays site. "I'll e-mail a letter outlining the accusations, Mr. Bollinger, but I strongly recommend you make yourself available to meet with us, as soon as possible."

As Bollinger moved away from the pontoon, two large green eyes appeared above the surface of the lake and watched him as he rushed away.

* * *

"Bloody hell, woman, you really are frustrating me. Which way do you want to go?"

Benjy Rumanackrin was checking some new data on Cyclone Nola. "Not this way you silly woman, go southeast, into the Tasman Sea why don't you. There's nothing out there but the southern ocean."

"How's it looking Benjy?" his supervisor asked.

"Not the best, boss, still a category one, and turning southwest."

"Shit, that's not good Benjy. A cyclone this far south can cause a lot of damage. What's the landfall?"

"Between the Gold Coast and Coffs Harbour, if it stays on its present course—in about forty-eight hours I'd reckon." Benjy flashed a broad grin. It was an infectious smile of sparkling white teeth against his dark skin. "But I wouldn't worry too much, boss. I think it'll be downgraded to a rain depression by the time it hits the coast."

"It looks a big bugger, Benjy."

Oh yes, boss. Take your umbrella with you if you're going up north," Benjy said, and chuckled at his own humour.

* * *

The following morning, Dwayne Gannet eased his truck up the steep incline along the well-worn fire track in the hills behind Serenity Quays. This was his third trip into the area in the past eight weeks, but this time Gannet was on a mission—a mission of revenge.

The call from a Council engineer was the catalyst for his anger. They had photographic evidence, he said, in a complaint submitted by a member of the public. The photograph showed him on his bobcat, vandalising a watercourse in the nature reserve behind Serenity Quays. His irresponsible actions, the complainant claimed, had undermined the creeks and waterways, which may have caused recent flooding in the resort. The Council advised him that they considered his conduct gravely irresponsible, and they would be placing the matter in the hands of the police.

When Gannet reached his destination, he sat in his vehicle and looked down on the almost deserted Serenity Quays, which was just visible in the morning haze. Gannet had quickly realised it would be Bollinger's word against his. The bastard had planned to set him up all along—that's why he had gone to the authorities with the photos. There was little doubt in Gannet's mind that Bollinger was the *member of the public* who had raised the complaint.

Now Dwayne Gannet was determined to do one thing. If he were going down, he would take Dermot Bollinger with him.

Gannet knew that if he was to shift the blame to Bollinger, he needed photographic evidence of his own, so he devised a simple plan. He would remove the soil from the creek embankment, as he had done previously, and take his own photographs of the work. He would also prepare a quotation, based on Bollinger's instructions—then he would throw himself at the mercy of the court and hope they would accept his story.

It was the final element of Gannet's plan that would give him the most pleasure. Bollinger had refused to pay him any extra money for restoring the creek wall, so when he finished later in the day, he would leave the creek wall open. Bollinger could find someone else to do the restoration work.

It was mid-morning as he hurried to unload the bobcat. He needed to remove the soil from the bank of the creek, and hope there was still enough light to take his photograph when he finished.

By late afternoon, Gannet realised he had little hope of completing the work as he'd planned. Most of the soil had been removed from the embankment, but he would need at least two more hours to finish the job. As Gannet looked to the sky, he could see heavy clouds beginning to move in over the mountain range. This caused him concern, because the resulting darkness would make working conditions difficult and dangerous.

He had no choice, he decided. He would leave the bobcat on site, and come back in the morning to complete the work.

As Gannet's truck rumbled back down the fire track, ominous black clouds gathered on the horizon.

Chapter Twenty-Five

The first rainsquall came around two in the morning. By dawn, fifty millimetres of rain had fallen, and Cyclone Nola, now a large rain depression, was only just reaching the coast.

Throughout the day, heavy rain, high winds, and lightning were causing chaos from Southeast Queensland to Newcastle, north of Sydney. No area was worse hit than the coastal region around Byron Bay and Ballina. Tides were higher than normal, and a huge sea swell was causing massive damage along the coastline.

At the same time as the tidal river rose to critical heights, a mass of water from the hills in the catchment area above Serenity Quays burst through the gaping hole in the wall of the largest creek. The water poured down the ancient watercourse like a giant waterfall, and into the resort's holding lake, which, in turn, flooded the canals.

By nightfall, as the river reached full tide, a wall of water almost two metres high rushed into the resort, taking everything in its path. The security gates were the first to go, found later a twisted mess, two hundred metres away. The twenty homes that still remained on the estate were in the early stages of being dismantled. Unshackled from their footings, they were unable to withstand the great surge of water, and were smashed to matchwood against one another. The underground power and sewerage network was destroyed, along with the resort's roads and pathways, while lawns, gardens, and other landscaping were buried under a tide of mud and silt. The next morning, Serenity Quays was a huge lake littered with floating palm trees and other debris.

Television breakfast programs ran the storm as their lead story. Live coverage was shown of the devastation to a residential

194

resort called Serenity Quays on the Far North Coast of New South Wales, where twenty homes had been inundated and washed away. No mention was made in the reports that the houses were partly dismantled, and the resort had been unoccupied for four weeks.

Forty-eight hours after the storm first hit, the sky cleared and most of the floodwaters receded, but the destruction left behind in Serenity Quays was devastating.

* * *

Immediately after the weather cleared, Davenport senior hired a helicopter to inspect, first hand, the damage to his newest acquisition. Because of Joshua's intense interest in the project, Davenport decided to take his son with him. He was extremely proud of Joshua for the enormous amount of research he had put into their new development at Serenity Quays. Also along for the ride, was Davenport Developments' corporate lawyer.

The first sweep over the site highlighted the devastation. With the second pass, there were concerned glances between the three men. As the helicopter returned to the base, they discussed their options.

"Your rider will certainly enable you to opt out of the contract, Joe," the lawyer said. "This land is obviously subject to flooding—serious flooding."

Joe Davenport looked at his son and placed a sympathetic hand on his arm. "I don't believe we have any choice, Joshua."

His son nodded in agreement, a look of disappointment on his face.

"What I can't understand, Joe," the lawyer shouted over the engine noise, "is why you toughened up the flood clause in the contract last month. That rider has probably saved your company millions."

"You should ask Joshua that question," Joe Davenport replied, pointing to his son. "He's the one who recommended the amendments."

The lawyer looked at Joshua inquiringly, but Joshua just shrugged and grinned.

On the helicopter's return journey to the Gold Coast, they implemented their course of action. The Act of God clause would be invoked, and the sale of Serenity Quays would not proceed. Within the hour, their solicitors were drawing up the necessary documents. The contract would be terminated, and there would be a request for the holding deposit to be returned.

* * *

The amount of water in and around Serenity Quays had caused alarm, and an investigation had begun immediately. An aerial inspection of the site by local authorities located a breach in the main watercourse above Serenity Quays. A ground inspection the same day identified the site specifically, and found clear evidence that the breach in the wall of the creek had been deliberately caused. The machinery responsible for the damage was, in fact, still parked at the site. Subsequent investigations by the police located the owner of the bobcat, who was arrested on a fire track a short distance away, beside his bogged vehicle. The man, identified as Dwayne Gannet, had apparently returned in his truck during the storm in an effort to retrieve the bobcat.

Most national networks reported the story that police had interviewed the owner of Serenity Quays, but no charges had been laid. As Bollinger inspected the site, a news crew from the local television station pursued him for his comments on the flooding. While he was in no mood to talk to the press, he couldn't resist the opportunity to be seen on national television.

"What did you feel when you saw the devastation in your resort, Mr. Bollinger?" the reporter asked.

Bollinger looked at the woman with disdain. How do you think I felt, you dumb bitch? he thought to himself. Bollinger removed his sunglasses, wiped his eyes, and looked directly at the camera. "Regardless of the huge financial loss my company has been burdened with today, I'm gladdened by the knowledge that none of my residents have suffered any physical or financial inconvenience."

Bollinger wiped his eyes again, then turned and walked away from the reporter and stood silently on his own, looking out over the devastation. That worked well, he thought, smiling smugly to himself.

The television cameras, which had caught every word of Bollinger's heart wrenching statement, panned away to several of Bollinger's mob. They had been organised earlier in the day to stand behind Bollinger and give him moral support. The camera settled on one person who had stood next to Bollinger the whole time, nodding enthusiastically at everything he said.

"You are a former resident of Serenity Quays?" the reporter asked the man.

"Yes I am," the interviewee replied.

"We understand there was no one living in the resort when the floodwaters hit," the reporter continued.

The interviewee fidgeted nervously. "Yes, that's correct. Mr. Bollinger was concerned for the safety of the residents of Serenity Quays, so several months ago he moved us all to another one of his resorts on the Tweed Coast—at his expense, I must add. As a result, we were spared what could have been a catastrophic incident." The interviewee looked towards Bollinger, still standing off on his own. "Mr. Bollinger is a great man, and everyone is thankful for his kindness and generosity, and for the concern he has shown towards the people in his care."

* * *

Trevor Albanyon sat upright in his lounge chair. He was enjoying a wine before dinner while he watched the evening news. He had listened with casual interest to the stories of Cyclone Nola's destructive path along the East Coast, when the name *Dermot Bollinger* caught his attention. As a Tax Office Investigator with the ATO in Brisbane, he was involved with an ongoing audit of Bollinger's financial affairs. But there was a missing link in the Bollinger investigations. A co-conspirator, needed to bring Bollinger to trial, had vanished five years earlier, before charges could be laid against him.

Albanyon watched the segment until it finished, then he picked up the telephone and called a Gold Coast number.

"Hello, Sam Gregan speaking." The sluggish response indicated to Albanyon that his work colleague had been taking a nap.

"Sam, it's Trev. I've found him. I've found Spencer J. Scraggs," he said, unable to contain his excitement.

"Spencer who?" Gregan asked, as he struggled to come awake.

"That phoney accountant who devised the fraudulent tax shelter for Dermot Bollinger, and the real estate agent you're chasing, what's his name—Fiddlemore? Scraggs was living just over the border, and all this time we thought he was dead." Albanyon sighed. "We're going to get that bastard, Sam, and when we do, we'll get his two mates."

Suddenly Gregan was wide-awake. "I want to be in on this one, Trev. I've waited a long time to get my hands on Mortimer Fiddlemore."

"I'll call into the office first thing in the morning and make the necessary arrangements. We'll need a warrant so the police can bring him in for questioning. How about I pick you up around eleven? We'll take a nice drive down the Tweed Coast and pay our friend Spencer J. Scraggs a visit."

* * *

Felicity Grimes stared in disbelief at the three men standing in front of her. One of them was a Federal Police Officer. The paint hadn't dried on the walls of her new manager's office at Hideaway Cove, and already she was experiencing her first police raid.

Felicity shook her head in disbelief. "Alright," she said sarcastically, "let me guess. You're here to arrest every resident at Hideaway Cove for pension card fraud?"

There was a confused look on Albanyon's face. "Actually, we *are* here on a fraud matter, Ms. Grimes, and it concerns a tenant of yours by the name of Spencer J. Scraggs. Would you direct us to his residence please?"

"Scraggs? You're here to arrest Spencer J. Scraggs?"

"That's right, Ms. Grimes. Now, can you give us the directions please?"

"This I've go to see," Felicity said, taking a large set of keys from her desk. "Come with me."

Scraggs' house was close to the office, and a few minutes later Felicity and the three men were standing on his front verandah. Felicity knocked several times, but there was no answer.

"You've just missed him," a voice behind them said. "He's gone."

Scraggs' next-door neighbour, George Mollitt, was sitting on his verandah watching them. A birdcage was sitting on a table next to him.

"Gone where?" the police officer asked.

Mollitt scratched his chin. "Dunno, just said he had to go someplace."

"So he didn't say exactly where he was going?"

"Nope, just tossed a bag in his car and took off," Mollitt replied.

The police officer was becoming impatient. "Did he say why he had to leave so suddenly?" he asked.

"Yeah." Mollitt scratched his chin again. "Said he got a call from an old work mate up in Brisbane—about some trouble that was brewin'."

The police officer looked at the old man suspiciously. "And that was it—he said nothing else?"

"Nope," the old man replied.

The police officer turned to walk back to the others waiting on Scraggs' verandah.

"There was one other thing, now that I think of it," Mollitt called to the policeman. The police officer turned quickly in anticipation. "He give me this here budgie—said I could keep it 'cause he wasn't coming back."

Chapter Twenty-Six

Gerry was surprised to see Joshua Davenport so dejected when they met several days after the devastating flood. Gerry knew that his business skills and experience were being utilised by the young man to win his father's affection, but he had not realised Joshua's passion for the Serenity Quays development.

"There'll be other projects, Joshua, and I'd be willing to put something else together for you under our existing arrangement," Gerry said.

"That's very good of you to offer, Gerry, but in the future you'll be paid your normal fee for any work you do for Davenport Developments." Joshua studied Gerry for a moment. "What made you mention the possibility of flooding in Serenity Quays, Gerry? That was weird."

Gerry shrugged. "A hunch, I guess."

"Well, thank God for hunches. It's a pity, though. I liked the concept," he said, a look of disappointment on his face.

"You were really committed to the Serenity Quays development, weren't you?" Gerry asked.

"Yes I was, Gerry, but as you say, others will come along that'll be just as challenging."

Gerry got up from his chair and walked to a large window that looked down onto the Gold Coat Highway, worming its way through the high-rise jungle of Surfers Paradise. "There may be another project that could be worth looking at, if you don't mind me making a suggestion."

"I'm interested in any suggestion you make, Gerry," Joshua responded.

"It's another of Bollinger's properties. This one's on the Tweed Coast, right on the beach, with a total of one hundred and seventy prefabricated homes in two subdivisions. It also has a fabulous nine-hole golf course and four bowling greens."

Sounds great, what's he asking?"

"Actually, the property isn't on the market, but Bollinger's in financial trouble, Joshua. That's why he was desperate to sell Serenity Quays. Now he stands to lose millions when they rezone the area—and they will. Council won't allow any more homes to be built on the site, now it's prone to serious flooding. He also has an expensive court case coming up."

Gerry returned to the desk. "Dermot Bollinger needs working capital to survive, Joshua, and I believe Davenport Developments has a great opportunity to take advantage of his predicament."

"Could we get a look at the place, without Bollinger knowing?" Joshua was having difficulty restraining his eagerness.

"I know someone who lives in the resort. He's a personal friend of mine, and he'd treat anything you discuss with him in the strictest confidence.

Joshua got to his feet and reached for his coat. "How about we go and have a look now?" he said, with his usual enthusiasm.

* * *

Wilfred Armadas Mutton was a large man with floppy jowls—the cause, his detractors claimed, was from grossly overeating. Amongst his peers, he was jokingly referred to as *Glutton Mutton*. The man also emitted a body odour that indicated a reluctance to bathe regularly, this brought about by his unwillingness to remove his legal robes. Some claimed he even wore his legal regalia to bed. But Mutton was one of Queensland's leading barristers, and the man Dermot Bollinger had chosen to defend him against what he claimed were outrageous and unsubstantiated charges.

Bollinger fidgeted nervously as he looked around the large conference chamber. His own solicitor, Harvey Steele, sat beside him. On the opposite side of the table, Mutton's support team watched their leader pace up and down as if he were the Messiah. The *situation room,* as Mutton called it, was richly carpeted. Drapes of gold brocade hung from large leadlight windows, and a huge chandelier adorned the ceiling. The furnishings were sumptuous, with genuine Edwardian chairs around a magnificent mahogany conference table, a prized piece of furniture in the opulent offices of *Mutton, Dubray and Toombs, Barristers at Law.*

Bollinger leant a little closer to his solicitor, Harvey Steele. "How much is this clown costing me?" he whispered.

"Around two thousand dollars an hour," Steele whispered back.

The room fell silent as Mutton cleared his throat and glared at the two men. He then turned and continued to pace the floor at one end of the great table—his thumbs tucked into his gown. To Mutton, even a routine meeting in his office was a prelude to a major court scene. Bollinger watched as the great man stopped and looked off into the distance. On his face was a pained and tormented expression, caused, Bollinger assumed, by the burden of legal responsibly that now confronted him. Finally, Mutton turned and looked around the room, and with all the aplomb and dignity his high office demanded, he passed wind very loudly.

Mutton adjusted his gown, and his gaze settled on Bollinger. He placed his hands on the table and leant forward towards his client. "Mr. Bollinger, I have just come from a meeting with some of my learned colleagues. We're trying to spare you an unpleasant court appearance."

Bollinger eased back in his chair. "Why should I have to defend myself in court? Gannet's the guilty party. He sabotaged my resort because he claimed I owed him money—which was a lie."

"I'm sure you are innocent of these accusations, Mr. Bollinger," Mutton said, with a wave of his arm. "But the courts may see it differently. It will be your word against his."

"I have photographic evidence," Bollinger insisted.

"There's other photographic evidence that's even more damaging, Mr. Bollinger, particularly if you go to trial," Mutton replied.

"Gannet took a photo of a breach in the creek wall, so what does that prove?"

"Someone else took photographs as well, Mr. Bollinger. More detailed and more incriminating than those taken by you, or Gannet," Mutton replied.

Bollinger swallowed nervously. "Someone else took photos—who?" he asked in a trembling voice.

"We're unable to ascertain that at the moment. The authorities won't say. What concerns my learned colleagues and me is the possibility that this third party may come forward if you go to trial, and give evidence against you."

Bollinger slumped back even further in his chair. "Jesus Christ," he said, nervously wiping his mouth with the palm of his hand. "What can we do?"

"All's not lost, Mr. Bollinger," Mutton said, as he untied the ribbon on a large folder in front of him. "The authorities appear willing to offer you a compromise."

"What sort of compromise?" Bollinger asked suspiciously.

"I'm not privy to that information, Mr. Bollinger; that matter is none of my business. But a colleague of mine has asked me to hand this letter to your solicitor." Mutton removed an envelope from the folder and slid it over to Steele, who opened it, and read the document inside.

"It seems the Council are expecting a donation of land," Steele said.

"What land?" Bollinger snapped.

Steele cleared his throat. "This letter is addressed to Bollinger Properties Pty Ltd, and dated today," he said. "'Council wishes to thank Mr. Dermot Bollinger for his extremely generous donation of that parcel of land known as Serenity Quays to the people of this shire. The Council wishes to advise that the land is subject to flooding, and is no longer suitable for residential development. At the next meeting of Council, the land will be rezoned public parkland. The Council also advises that, in view of this generous donation, no charge of misconduct or damages would be sought against the former owner of Serenity Quays.'"

Bollinger placed his head in his hands. Three weeks ago he was happily negotiating the sale of Serenity Quays for twenty-two million dollars. Now it was worth nothing, rezoned a park. The land was useless—he may as well accept their compromise. The last thing he needed was an expensive and time-consuming court case.

"Well, Mr. Bollinger?" Mutton asked impatiently.

"It seems I have little choice in the matter."

"I think you're doing the wisest thing, Mr. Bollinger," Mutton said.

"And exactly when did I make this generous donation of my land to Council?" Bollinger asked in a cynical tone.

"Why, just yesterday morning, Mr. Bollinger," Mutton replied, sliding a second envelope over to Steele.

"I assume you know nothing about the contents of that letter either?" Bollinger muttered sarcastically.

There was a smirk on Mutton's face. "Absolutely no idea," he said. "But I suggest you sign it before you leave this morning, so we can wrap this matter up."

* * *

"Look dear," Bollinger's wife said, "your friend Davenport is on local television."

Bollinger waved his dinner fork at the television set. "Davenport's no friend of mine," he muttered.

Bollinger and his wife had decided to stay over on the Gold Coast and celebrate the sale of Hideaway Cove. Not that there was a lot to celebrate. Davenport had screwed him down to less than fourteen million dollars in order to achieve a quick settlement. The land alone was worth that, Bollinger had grumbled constantly to his wife during the brief negotiations.

"Things are going to change," he said to her, ignoring the television interview. "Now I have working capital again, I've made myself a promise. From now on, there'll be no more *Mr. Nice Guy*—I intend to be much more ruthless in my business dealings in future."

Mrs. Bollinger rolled her eyes, then turned her attention back to the television interview.

"Is this a new direction your company intends to take, Mr. Davenport?" the television reporter asked.

"Not really. My son liked the idea, and feels there are opportunities for us in this area, but our main aim was to help out a business associate. The Bollinger organisation has gone through some difficult times recently, as you know."

"Will your son run the resort, Mr. Davenport?"

"No, my son is going to be too busy in other areas of the company's business." He placed his arm around his son's shoulder. "I'm pleased to announce that, effective immediately, Joshua Davenport will become a full member of our Board of Directors."

Davenport continued, still gripping his son's shoulder. "Joshua has been very wise in appointing a General Manger to control our new acquisition, a man with a great deal of experience within this industry." Davenport directed the cameras to his left, and Gerry's smiling face appeared on the screen. "That man is Mr. Gerry Curry."

Mrs. Bollinger was startled by an angry growl that erupted behind her. "Davenport's office!" Bollinger screamed. "That's where I saw you…"

Suddenly, everything became clear to Dermot Bollinger, and he was filled with an uncontrollable rage. He drew back his arm, hurled his glass of Cheval Regis at the television screen, and the smiling face of Gerry Curry exploded in a shower of glass, whisky, and a puff of smoke.

Epilogue

Two months later…

Dwayne Gannet agreed to meet the officer from the Sheriff's Office on site at Serenity Quays. After two months, the recovery team, which had worked under Gannet's supervision, had created a magnificent wetland for the local bird life. Now the work was finished, and so was Gannet's sentence of three hundred hours community service. On the block of land where Alby Titmus' house once stood, Gannet and the officer finalised his release. The office signed a form and passed a copy to Gannet.

"You're free to go, Mr. Gannet, now you've completed your three hundred hours."

Gannet took the form and stuffed it in his pocket. "Gee thanks," he muttered sarcastically. "Should I send a thank-you card to the Magistrate?"

The officer smiled. "You're lucky he didn't send you to jail."

"For what I did?" Gannet scoffed. "If you ask me, New South Wales is a police state."

"Well, you've done a good job cleaning up this mess; the place looks fantastic." The officer opened his car door and threw his clipboard on the passenger seat. "What do you plan to do now?"

"I'll fly back to Brisbane tonight, and hope I can salvage what's left of my business there."

"Can I give you a lift to the airport?"

Gannet glanced out across the shimmering waters of the lake. It had been a hot day and the water looked inviting. "No thanks, I need to clean up a bit." He held up his mobile phone. "I'll ring for a cab."

When the officer had gone, Gannet stripped off his clothes and placed them on the bank. Then he waded out into the water.

On the opposite side of the lake, two large, sinister green eyes suddenly broke the surface and moved slowly towards the swimmer, who was enjoying himself in the cool waters of the lake...

* * *

A week later, a tradesman put the final touches to a sign that he had erected near the lake. After the work was finished, he knelt down on the bank to wash his hands, and he noticed some clothes lying in the grass nearby. Inside the bundle of clothes he found a wallet and a mobile phone. He looked around to see if anyone was watching, then removed the money from the wallet. He then threw the wallet and the clothing in the back of the truck with the other rubbish. He checked the phone, saw that it was working, and placed it, and the money, in his pocket.

The tradesman looked around again, then he got into his vehicle and quickly sped away, scattering dirt and stones over his newly erected sign, which read: *Welcome to Serenity Quays Nature Reserve.*

Below that, hung another sign: *Please don't feed the wildlife.*

Acknowledgements

I would like to thank my dear friends Doug and Libby Lee for their support and encouragement, and Jean D. Briggs and Carole Woods for their advice and assistance.